T0084412

The Voice of the River

Also by Melanie Rae Thon

*In This Light*

*Sweet Hearts*

*First, Body*

*Iona Moon*

*Girls in the Grass*

*Meteors in August*

# THE VOICE OF THE RIVER

## MELANIE RAE THON

FC2

TUSCALOOSA

Published by FC2, an imprint of The University of Alabama Press,
with support provided by the Publishing Program at the University of
Houston–Victoria.

Address all editorial inquiries to: Fiction Collective Two, University of Houston–
Victoria, School of Arts and Sciences, Victoria, TX 77901-5731

Cover and book design: Lou Robinson
Typefaces: Jenson and Thousand Sticks
Produced and printed in the United States of America
∞
The paper on which this book is printed meets the minimum requirements of
American National Standard for Information Sciences—Permanence of Paper for
Printed Library Materials, ANSI Z39.48–1984

**Library of Congress Cataloging-in-Publication Data**

Thon, Melanie Rae.
 The voice of the river : a novel / by Melanie Rae Thon.—1st ed.
  p. cm.
 ISBN 978-1-57366-162-1 (pbk. : alk. paper)—ISBN 978-1-57366-826-2 (electronic)
 1. Life—Fiction. I. Title.
 PS3570.H6474V65 2011
 813'.54—dc22
                    2010053839

*for all who share the mystery and miracle*
*of life on earth*

*The voice of the river that has
emptied into the Ocean
Now laughs and sings just like
God.*

*~Hafiz*

# Contents

## Part Three

## Part Four

# List of Names

This abbreviated list of names is arranged by family connection and/or other intimate association.

Kai Dionne, age 17
Talia, Kai's dog
Lela (Hayes) Dionne, Kai's mother, divorced from Kai's father, Tim
Christine Hayes, Kai's aunt, Lela's sister, divorced from Kai's uncle, Roy McKenna
Griffin Hayes, Kai's uncle, Lela's brother
Theo Hayes, Kai's grandfather, Lela's father
Naomi Bonalee Hayes, Kai's grandmother, Lela's mother, no longer living

Tulanie Rey McKenna, age 17, Kai's cousin, paralyzed in bicycle accident
Iris Jenae McKenna, age 13, Kai's cousin
Christine (Hayes) McKenna (Delacroix), Kai's aunt, divorced from Roy and remarried
Roy McKenna, Kai's uncle

Timothy (Tim) Dionne, Kai's father, divorced from Lela

Angie Dionne, Tim's second wife

Juliana, age 9; and Roxie, age 7: Tim and Angie's daughters,
    Kai's half-sisters

Vale Dionne, Tim's brother, no longer living


Dorrie (Teodora) Esteban, no longer living, the girl Kai and
    Tulanie love together

Elia Esteban, Dorrie's brother, no longer living

Oleta (Riero) Esteban, Dorrie and Elia's mother

Mario Esteban, Oleta's husband, Dorrie and Elia's father

Amalita, Oleta's child who was never born


Daniel Sidoti, the piano tuner who believes he will find Kai

Denise Sidoti, Daniel's wife

Clare and Nora Sidoti, Daniel and Denise's young daughters


Arlo Dean, a man who was in prison with Roy McKenna,
    the one who finds Talia

Lucie Dean, Arlo's mother

Vernon Dean, Arlo's father, no longer living


Peter Fleury (who calls himself No), a homeless boy
    searching for Kai

Neville Kane, a homeless boy, loved by Oleta Esteban

Trina Matteas, a homeless girl, a friend of Tulanie Rey

Rikki Kruse, a homeless girl, befriended by Mario Esteban

Tejano, one of the stray dogs who lives with the children

[Oleta Esteban and Arlo Dean and Tulanie Rey McKenna
are all involved with the homeless children.]

Joseph Trujillo, a homeless man Tulanie Rey meets in the
hospital after his bicycle accident
Vincent Flute, a man who almost dies when his truck rolls
and catches fire
Willis and Louise Brodie, the elderly couple who save
Vincent

PRELUDE

# Love Song for Tulanie Rey

*The breaking away of childhood left you intact. In a moment
you stood there, as if completed by a single miracle, all at once.*

*~Rainer Maria Rilke*

Tulanie was broken. You loved your cousin before you were born, each in his mother's womb, wordless and perfect. You leapt in joy, pushed hard with feet and fists whenever the sisters laughed together. Laughter was the first sound, a fluttery tender trill, birdsong under water. You lived inside the sound, and knew love as pure vibration.

Then you were five and he was five, and love was a winter night, smell of pine, crackling fire. Love: a dark room with cold windows, you and Tulanie Rey rubbing feet fast on carpet to make sparks jump between your fingers. Tulanie sparked the white cat, the crib where Iris slept, his own ears, the television's long antennae.

He was dangerous, your cousin: eight years old and flinging himself from roof to snowbank—ten, and making you climb the high cedar fence to swim naked in Mearl Everly's pool.

He was never sorry for anything. When Aunt Christine smacked his butt, he turned the other cheek, said, *Hit me harder.*

Some days he refused all words and spoke in the voice of the cat, the loon, the river. He carved signs on himself or threw stones at your window. He stood mute in the freezing rain—he was the rain—waiting for you to run into the woods and find him.

You turned eleven, wild with love, both falling in love with Dorrie Esteban together. Dark-eyed Dorrie gave you each a curl of her black hair tied with green ribbon, and later, swaying in her tree house, she showed you the violet scars high on her hipbones. Leaves whispered, and you wanted to speak now in their language. Dorrie said, *That's where the doctor took marrow from me and gave it to Elia, my brother.* But little Elia Esteban died anyway, and now Dorrie was going to die too, because she didn't save him.

You imagined the dark place inside her bones, hollow needle long enough to probe, sharp lance twisting to the center. You saw Dorrie's deep gold core pulled into a syringe and pumped into her brother. Light spilled through the slats of the tree house, and you wanted to touch Dorrie where the light touched and be that silent.

Then she did die, just as she'd promised, the next year, a car accident with her mother. Oleta Esteban said Dorrie kept her eyes open for the longest minute, and she could feel her there, everywhere, as if Dorrie were the air—Dorrie the light, fractured through the windshield.

Oleta took a hard breath, and Dorrie closed her eyes and

became very small, the air inside her mother, and Oleta said, *I wasn't afraid of anything, and I didn't hurt—I just felt Dorrie there, in me, very peaceful.*

Later, Oleta Esteban hurt all the time. She couldn't walk more than half a block without weeping, feet crushed from slamming brakes that didn't stop them. How many bones can you break in one foot, one face, one body? She looked inside herself and saw all her bones crumbling.

It hurt to breathe into the space where five fractured ribs mended. Even after the bruises disappeared and the cuts on her face and hands healed, forever after, she could never take a full breath, never bear to fill her lungs and feel them huge inside her—never, though Doctor Savoy looked so pleased, so immaculately satisfied, showing her and her husband Mario the X ray, saying, *Your ribs are perfect,* proud, as if he alone had worked this miracle, slipped his bright white hands inside to hold her bones while she lay dreaming.

Mario squeezed her hand, and his touch hurt her fingers, her whole arm, her face, her pelvis. It hurt to go home with him—husband, stranger—to be inside the tiny house where she was the mother of no children. It hurt to be in the yard, to sit in the cradle of the swing, though she was small enough now, thin as her own daughter.

It hurt to hear dogs barking. God had done this to her, because of the child lost, the one wished away long ago, the secret never spoken. Oleta Riero, fourteen years old, watching the dark clots of herself swirl down the toilet—down and gone, back to God, the dirt, the crows, the river. If not for cramps so fierce they crippled her, if not for the fact that she fell when

5

she tried to stand and struck her head on the toilet—if not for Donia Chavez finding her there locked in the little stall half an hour later—if not for stained underpants twisted around her knees and strays in the schoolyard howling—if not for those two hungry, sore-skinned dogs following her home that day, sniffing, she might have said it was a dream, a lie, impossible: just dark clots and bright blood, not a child flushed and now down the river floating.

You wanted to tell Oleta Esteban about the day you and Tulanie touched Dorrie's scar, and she told you she was going to die, and she wasn't afraid, as if it were a thing of the past and not a thing to fear in the future. Dorrie said, *Sometimes I see myself walking toward myself, and I just feel very beautiful.*

You wanted to knock on the Estebans' door, but you were afraid of the skinny woman inside, how old she looked, how shriveled. Afraid of the red curtain always drawn closed across the front window. Afraid of the chicken in the yard, bigger than the three little dogs yapping. Afraid of the black rooster and the white goat with no ears and the sheep on a long chain and the man, this father of no children, who drove away in his rusty blue truck every morning, but who might return on foot, in silence, and open the door, and find you there, and kill you.

The thrush in the woods behind Oleta's house held one shimmering note so bright and clear you thought the bird would shatter—and then it did shatter: into a heart-sparking ripple of song that split down your bones and burst from your body.

Tulanie Rey McKenna turned fifteen nine days before you did, and so you were only fourteen the day you saw your cousin broken. He rode his bike too fast, whipped down the ravine at night, jolted through the gully, howling. Tulanie wanted to die, he said, a joke between you. He whooped and barked, motherless boy, wild dog on wheels. Nobody waited at home to smack him. Aunt Christine was three times gone, and now gone for good, married to a prison guard in Deer Lodge, a man she met the year Uncle Roy was an inmate.

The day it happened was just a day like any other, a hot day in August, and for once Tulanie was riding very slowly, eyes closed, no hands, his latest trick, a test of nerves and balance, and he must have heard the car, but it was too late to swerve, too late for Ross Freyle to tap the brakes, and the old man rolling out of his driveway clipped Tulanie's rear tire, and the bike skidded into the street and the boy you loved flew and you saw him, but you were not afraid because you'd seen him fly from tree and swing and rooftop. You'd seen him rise up from grass, snow, water. You'd gazed down from the roof to see him lying on his back in the snow, moving arms and legs, making himself into an angel. You teetered at the edge, and he tempted you without words, only with laughter—he made you leap; he made you follow—and you were both alive that day, so why should this be any different?

He flew twenty feet and now lay very still, limbs splayed, but so peaceful, and you walked toward the place where he lay as if you were walking toward yourself, your body in his body, very beautiful. Light falling through leaves moved as the leaves moved, and you were the light between leaves tenderly touching him.

Then the old man touched you, muttering, and his car roared, stopped still but still running, and the light through leaves broke and you saw yourself and the trembling man and Tulanie in fragments, and you were afraid, fractured by light, cold where the man's cold hand touched you.

You thought his heart would burst from his body, that his red heart would fall into your hands, and you wouldn't know what to do or how to slip it back inside, and he'd die right there, his chest an open mouth, his dark heart throbbing in your hands, and you kneeling with the weight of it.

It was true what you saw: Ross Freyle did die, four months later. Ross Freyle fell down his basement stairs and lay in the dark on the cool concrete three days before his brother found him.

But Tulanie didn't die. Tulanie woke the day you turned as old as he was. He spoke his first words to you: *Touch my legs*, he said. *Can you feel them?*

Now when you go to the skate park together, Tulanie curls his limp legs under him to ride his board down the gentlest slope while his little sister Iris smokes cigarettes or pops wheelies in his wheelchair. Wild dog Tulanie Rey McKenna waits at the bottom for you to come and push him up the other side so he can roll down again, and rock there in the middle. Clouds pass, but you are not afraid of the light or lack of it: you love the light as it gathers and breaks you over and over.

PART ONE

# I

## SAVIORS

Talia paces the dark hallway. If Kai doesn't get her out soon, the whimpering will start and then the yelping. Frost on the windows this morning, cold air from Canada moving down the Rockies. The boy would like to sleep another hour, but he promised long ago she'd never need to howl again if he could help it.

He loved the shivering dog the moment she saw him. Five years now, and Talia was going to die that day if he didn't take her. Half-starved, half-wild, two years old and not housebroken: the dog cowered in her cage, *Talia*, a tattered rag, long gray hair thin and tangled.

Kai's mother wanted him to love the sweet spaniel or faithful shepherd. She wanted him to take the little black terrier who danced on his hind legs like a tiny bear at the circus. But the girl with one blue eye and one gold-flecked hazel chose him, and he heard her name as if she spoke it.

Talia was afraid of the leash, afraid of the collar. She'd been smacked too many times, chained in the yard all night in winter. Kai's mother locked him out one day. He couldn't remember how long—fifteen minutes or five hours—but he did remember how cold he was as he ran door to door, window to window, trying to break into his own house, trying to see his own mother. Six years old, a lifetime ago. He wanted to forgive her even now, but she pretended to forget and never said that she was sorry.

In the house where Talia lived before his house, the bad dog shredded the pillows and drank from the toilet, pissed on the bed and dumped the garbage. She growled at the crawling baby. And why not? The little girl grabbed Talia's long hair and pulled, or climbed on top of her when she was sleeping.

Eight days before Kai found her at the shelter, Talia nipped one soft baby hand. Now the condemned dog had four hours left to live in exile. The baby's bright-eyed mother said, *If the gun had been in the kitchen drawer and not in my husband's glove box, I would have killed the bitch, I swear it.*

The baby wailed but did not bleed, and the mother dragged Talia into the yard and whacked her face with the chain as she hooked it. She never said the dog's name. She didn't know it.

Kai did not own Talia any more than his mother owned him or his grandfather owned the river. He loved her because she wanted to live. Talia chose him and spoke her name and shivered. He was twelve that day, and she was two. The dancing terrier could go home with any child, but this torn animal needed Kai, and only he could save her.

She's housebroken now, seven years old and mostly patient,

but her howl could still pierce the dark and wake his mother. He thinks of his cousin Tulanie Rey, paralyzed more than two years, what a privilege it is to walk in snow, a mystery and a miracle to go out in the world and move without wheels. He whispers, *Shush, I'm coming*, and the dog lets out a shivery cry, already joyful.

Theo hears Talia's voice. He has ten minutes at most if he hopes to walk with his grandson. He loves the beginning of day: the cold, the quiet, the dark hour before the boy goes to school and the dog spends the day mourning him.

The question for Theo this day and every day is not one of will and desire, but of hips and knees, hands that can or cannot pull on pants, fingers that can zip and button. He's too proud to ask any seventeen-year-old boy to help him. Across town, Theo's other grandson wakes and touches his legs, and does not know them. Tulanie sees the dark shape of the chair beside the bed. *This dream is mine. This dream is real.* Sleep is better. Sometimes the legs are gone, and Tulanie floats free without them, up the stairs and out the window. *Like smoke*, he says, *soon enough, some day.* He's not afraid. *What could be more strange than this?* Stone, air, water.

Last fall, a one-legged man pulled another man from a truck on fire. Theo remembers the photograph of Willis Brodie in the paper, left pant leg rolled to expose his prosthesis. The crippled savior is a spur, a spark, a reminder of a thousand failures. He remembers Louise Brodie holding her husband's arm, smiling like a girl, gazing up at him with adoration. You could see how they were: more in love each day after forty-nine years together. Behind them, their little house appeared, a tiny tilted log cabin sinking into the earth south of Coram. They were poor, yes, but their front window reflected tall pines and open sky, a whole world.

The man Brodie saved had a pregnant wife and three children. Willis and Louise had driven down to Polson that day, sixty-six slow miles to celebrate the wonder of Brodie's birthday. He'd almost died in January, knocked flat in the snow, heart clenched and nearly strangled. *Chopping wood*, he said, *like a fool*. Now he had a pacemaker and three bypasses. Little brother Sam played mandolin, and cousin Marty sang, ragged as Johnny Cash, then tenderly as Elvis. In praise, in gratitude, Willis pulled the sweetest sound he'd ever heard from his harmonica. They were old men, but they still knew how to whoop and laugh, how to let the song be the spark that set their sweet old bodies humming.

Nine days before he saw Vincent Flute's truck on fire, Willis Brodie couldn't even walk, hot wires of pain in the hip of his half-leg strung so tight they left him weeping. Two shots of cortisone had him in his shoes again. *Ambulatory*, he said, *my life is perfect*.

The Brodies headed home at dusk and were fifteen miles up the lake shore when they spotted the rolled truck sparkling. Three drivers passed ahead of them. Almost dusk now, so Willis couldn't say for sure whether they'd noticed the vehicle down the ditch and the shadow of a man dangling.

*Dead or alive*, Willis said, *I couldn't leave him*. Brodie wavered at the crest of the gully just long enough to speak to his legs. *You're going down there whether you want to or not*. Don't ask him how. There's no logical explanation.

Vincent Flute was alive, but not conscious, thirty-eight years old, 216 pounds, trapped in the cab, flames flickering around him. He hung upside down—no chance Brodie was going to yank him out that smashed window. *Then the battery sparked and Louise yelled my name and the flames doubled and I thought, yes, this is how hell will be in winter, face fried and backside frozen.* Vincent woke—just enough, just a little—and Brodie said, *I need your help, sir.*

*So polite, as if he were the one in trouble.* His sweetness amazed the man on fire. Flute unhooked his seat belt and crawled through jagged glass as the old man pulled and Louise yelled: *Run*, as if running were possible. *Sometimes a single word can save you.* The staggering pair reached the highway thirty seconds before the gasoline exploded. Louise helped Willis roll Vincent onto their tailgate, and together they wrapped the slumbering man in a blanket. Flute was out cold now, totally depleted.

Two more drivers passed, but the third one stopped and this one had a cell phone. Louise whispered, *It's okay. We're safe now.* The ambulance took seventeen astonishing minutes. Willis and Louise sang the whole time, soft and low, sweet rock-a-bye love songs, as if the man were their first and last and most belovéd only child. Vincent survived with cuts from the glass and bruises from impact, broken collarbone and dislocated shoulder, burns on his face and hands, and yes, he might have a few scars to show his friends, a white flame from throat to ear, but nothing serious.

Willis Brodie had saved Flute's parents and sisters, his brother and wife, six nieces, five nephews, the child in the womb and the children walking in the world, all who loved

Vincent Flute now, and all who might learn to love one another in the future. Brodie had torn the veil of despair, altered the inevitable. If God couldn't get the man out on his own, one-legged, seventy-three-year-old, heart-stuttering Willis Brodie would have to help him.

Theo wanted to be glad, but the photograph, Louise Brodie's tender gaze, pierced him. *She won't, not ever, his Naomi.* He can't let go of it, and when he thinks of Willis Brodie this morning, he slaps his own legs and says, *Get going.* He will have this day, one more day, to walk with Kai and Talia.

Talia bounds ahead of Kai and his grandfather. She's a narrow slash of animal, face sharp, hips bony, a long-legged leaping dog, some strange, wild crossbreed. All these years she's been trying to teach the boy what she knows about the world. She wants him to sense the white hare sitting still in snow, ears twitching. He's quick—five seconds and he's gone, two hundred feet beyond her. Talia wants Kai to understand that when they walk in dark woods, the great horned owl watches them. He'll kill a dog, a cat, a skunk, a porcupine—rip the hide off a fallen cow, snatch a coyote. Nothing is beyond his grasp: only the whirling hawk or a congregation of crows makes him flee in frenzy.

Talia moves fast when she feels the owl's golden eyes turn toward her. Her footsteps are thunderous to him, her breath a wild roaring. The hunched bird perches high in snagged branches, ready for a day's sleep, belly full of other creatures.

Why can't Kai smell the red fox? The scent of him makes Talia crazy. She wants to kill or chase or love him, lie down in the musty maze of his den and hide and wait there. It's easy enough to find: he's left a pile of wings and bird bones.

The boy's poverty, his stunning lack of awareness, spares him certain dangers: barbed quills in the face or searing sulfur spray harsh enough to blind him. Talia knows a burn worse than barbs, a smell so fierce she thought she'd die from it.

But fear is just another word for sorrow, and she wants to lead Kai to the dark cave where the black bear has borne two young in her miraculous slumber. Crawling on hands and knees, the boy could slip into the mouth of the cave and enter the world's deepest secret. Why doesn't he follow? The two weigh less than a pound together. He could hold a cub in each palm, let them suckle his salty fingers. This is where love begins, with pity and with laughter. Talia could take him to the cave, today, now, this very morning.

Why does he call her name? Why does he resist her?

The boy is so far behind, almost blind in early morning, lost between wisps of fog along the river—a graceful, long-limbed human child, fast in his way, but oh, not nearly, not ever as fast as Talia. He calls again, and she loves him, and she wants to wait, to obey, but the smell of all these living beings in the woods, and the sweet warm blood of ones just killed, and the cold air she sucks down her lungs, and her own dark blood pulsing from her wild heart just as the river pulses wild from its mysterious source are too tempting and too strong.

Sometimes Kai believes he is fully awakened, that Talia has restored his senses, resurrected him from the cave of human misconception. He believes he hears the mouse tunneling beneath snow just as she does, that he can leap and dig and catch it. Then Talia, his benevolent teacher, leads him a long mile into the woods, to the place where a whitetail deer fell three days ago, where her blood has frozen in the snow, and blood and ice are all that's left of her. Last November Talia did this, and Kai realized she had sensed the place from the road, followed a trail through trees, as if the frozen blood still trembled.

And it was true, the place was sacred. The doe turned in his mind as if in memory: her eyes opened wide, and she gave herself to him. The voice of the gun was his heart hammering, and his shoulder hurt where the butt kicked back against him. Tamarack and fir hummed, singing the story. Talia had found her way through a thousand other smells: spruce and pine, smoke and raven. He is nothing compared with her, a fumbling foolish human idiot. She loves him even in his crushing failure. For all she knows through her spectacular senses, she remains oblivious to shame and wonder. She is a dog, a creature, splendidly alive in every moment, purely joyful to eat pink snow and share this holy mystery. Kai wants to kneel and eat with her, let the blood of the deer become part of his body, but he is afraid of love so vast and silent.

Today Talia runs along the river, keen on the trail of an invisible squirrel. Only Kai's voice touches her. Theo follows far behind, struggling in snow, breaking through the frozen crust, dragging his heavy boots back to the surface, walking a dozen careful slippery steps, then breaking through again, but walking—walking on his arthritic legs, thankful for this small mercy, the gift of another day, a boy in the world who loves him, who turns to wait long enough for the blue beam of Theo's flashlight to catch him in the mist of fog, to illuminate his willowy human shape there in the trees at the edge of the river.

## 2

## THE RED FOX

Father, son, hungry dog—Lela wants them home and with her. She cracks six eggs in the red bowl, starts nine fat sausages sizzling. She's listening for Talia at the door, the dog's impatient yipping. Her father will want his coffee black in a light mug with a big handle, the green one easy to grip and lift with crippled fingers. Kai likes his half milk and chocolate. She's on her second bitter cup, dangerously buzzed, already jittery. She'll be sorry later, at the hospital, trying to tap a vein, hands trembling. She worked thirteen hours yesterday, eight drawing blood and collecting urine, five more driving the hotel shuttle. Today will be the same, Saturday just the shuttle—Sunday to shop and clean, Monday to Wednesday just the hospital.

*Where are you?* Lela folds a flowered napkin at each place, scarlet poppies for Kai, a tangle of tiny edelweiss for Theo. The violet bellflowers are hers, always, bloom into bloom, silent bleeding. She remembers Mother sewing these, two of each kind, stashing them in a drawer for thirty years, saving them for something special. She took them out at last, after she survived the night with the red fox, twenty-seven bites, six rounds of shots for rabies.

Theo saved Naomi from the fox, batted it with a stick, smashed its skull with a rock, weeping. She'd gone to the river to sleep alone. One more blessèd night: *As long as the water talks, I need to listen.* What choice did he have? No word Theo spoke could stop her.

She'd slept there with Griffin, a thousand and one nights on a narrow bed in the silver trailer, because the boy refused to sleep in his father's house, refused to speak his father's language.

*Why hurt me now? Isn't our son good and grown, safe on his mountain?*

Theo waited till dawn to walk through the woods, to bring bread and jam, cream and coffee. He found Naomi entwined with the red fox. They'd wrestled since dusk, twelve hours. She'd been sitting on the top step, *watching the light go, so peaceful,* and the little fox slipped from the woods and stood in the light as if to show her how beautiful he was. *A gift, you are, some mysterious consolation.* His fur caught the last rays, red and radiant. *Nothing between us now, no difference.* He was becoming light, all light, moving toward her.

*Is this love?*

The fox leaped as if to answer. He bit and clawed, knocked her to the ground, and she heard the brittle snaps of hip and elbow. He ran away, but came back, and bit again— face and arms and bare ankles. The sun had set; he was all animal. Sometimes he rested, weary beside her. Every time she twitched, he pounced again and bit more fiercely. She couldn't kill the fox because her hands were too small and her arms too weak and her elbow broken. She couldn't rise and run. The pain in her hip seared her. She couldn't see, glasses out of reach, in the dirt behind her. Finally she clutched the hissing fox to try to calm or comfort it—and he was calmer this way, and he did tear less hard, and he did bite less often.

That's how Theo found her. He struck the creature a dozen times with a stick and finally used a flat rock to crush his skull. The old man wept and flailed. He saw how Naomi pitied the fox even now as he killed him. He hated the broken body of the animal, its coat dull with dust, its blood on his own face spattered.

*I'm glad you came,* Naomi said, as if to call him back and save him.

Naomi Bonalee Hayes survived broken hip and fractured elbow, a hundred and twelve stitches, skin so fragile it tore, flesh that bruised no matter how tenderly you touched her. She surfaced from pneumonia in both lungs though Lela heard her slowly drowning.

So tiny Naomi was, eighty-three pounds when she came home to Theo four months later. *Your bride,* she said, showing him purple scars on neck and face, arms and ankles. She never again insisted on a night's peace, never walked half a mile through the woods to sleep by the river. Theo paid to have the silver trailer hauled away. *Scrap,* he said, *please take it.* The man who came had no wife, five children. Now, where the tin house stood, the forest grows green and wild.

*Safe*, Theo thought.

*You can't watch me every minute.*

But he did watch, winter to spring, Naomi out in the garden again, whispering to her columbine, snipping fast and apologizing to her roses. One bright August day, she was too weak to stand. *I can walk*, she said, *but not now, not right this minute.* She lay on the couch all afternoon, window open wide, white curtain billowing. A meadowlark sang from across the field. *Sit down, old man, listen.* The bird had a voice like a flute, seven wild notes rising up and then five more, sweetly falling. Why sing like this with mating over? Pure joy, pure confusion—a day so warm anything was possible. Theo wouldn't sit, not with her, this way. *Mister Busy.* She heard him sweeping the porch, scouring the toilet, sanding the broken chair, cursing at the noisy kettle.

The next morning, she was up and dressed long before Theo woke and wondered. He found her out in the garden again, digging potatoes. *It's time*, she said, *they're ready.*

He saw two rows of strange, misshapen bodies, potatoes drying in the dirt, some small and hard as shrunken plums, some swollen fat as golden melons. She had beans to pick, the last thirteen ears of corn to gather. *Get to work, old man, or leave me.* Everything he touched scared him. The tomatoes hung patiently on the vine, gloriously red, too bright and heavy, so warm in his hands he felt them growing.

Dizzy, yes, when she stood—but so was Theo. She watched him stoop and stagger. *Weary from the weight of me.* He turned as if her thought hurt him. *A bag of beans weighs more than you do.*

The second day of November, Theo followed Naomi Bonalee to the meadow where she left food for bears, starved that year, too hungry to hibernate. Hadn't she learned anything from the red fox?

*Let me go, old man—they won't hurt me.*

Pumpkins, eggs, fish, apples—she couldn't carry enough food for even one to sleep through winter. *There are a hundred in these woods, a thousand in the hills waiting.*

He wanted to help her that evening. *In and out of the tub, let me.* Why hide from Theo now? He'd loved her through every decade of her life. Clouded eye, wrinkled belly—he knew every scar and bone—*with my own eyes, with my own fingers.*

But no, not this way—she wouldn't let him see her splayed in the tub, *your wasted wife,* naked. She refused to call his name when she slipped—*just as you imagined.* There was nothing to feel: no bump on the back of the head, no split skin, no thick blood in warm water swirling. *Fine, I am— I'll just rest here a few minutes.* Torn vessels deep in the brain began to bleed, and a bruise bloomed, silent in its own dark swelling. She didn't tell him as they lay in bed, though she felt it now, the steady throbbing. She couldn't bear all the fuss and worry, another trip to town, another night in the hospital where they'd poke and prod, jab her with needles, hold their fingers up, ask, *How many?*

Naomi Bonalee didn't confess the next day though her hands were too weak to hold a cup of tea steady. *Not hungry,* she said, and even these words were hard to find and put together. *What now?* Theo thought, and used his own silence to punish her.

She never thought, *I'm dying*, until she was—in the absolute dark inside and outside—and she woke hours before dawn into a day she'd never see—and she wanted to speak his name, but couldn't, and the word pulsing in her head was *now*, and the last word was *Theo*.

*Subdural hematoma.* At the end of time there will be a language for everything, two words to pound through an old man's head over and over. *Nothing you could do*, Doctor Luria said, but Theo can list a thousand ways he failed her.

Theo hasn't caught Kai in the light for ten minutes, but he hears him call Talia, voice urgent. He can't see the squirrel skitter across thin ice, doesn't imagine the joyful dog flying after it, hears only the boy's cry, *No*, and the sound of ice like glass shattering. Kai sees the dog swept down and under, too impossible to believe, and he doesn't believe, not exactly— doesn't stop to think—only loves and leaps and follows, slides out onto the ice and crashes through it. Theo so far away, so blind to what is happening, feels the sudden shock, the cold water a heart-stopping jolt as sharp ice cuts through him. He runs as an old man runs: stumbling, falling, rising up, limping, hobbling, fanning the woods with light, hoping, knowing, calling, *Kai, Talia*, gasping.

# 3

## RIKA, MARIKA

*Love Song for Griffin*

What did Griffin say? *Those with hope survive.* You remember a story he told, a child pulled out and revived after three hours. Griffin will come, Griffin will save you. *Jab your knife or keys in the ice. Pull yourself half way out. Don't be afraid. Let your clothes drain. Those who despair vanish. Kick your feet. Pull slowly. Get your belly up on the ice. Stay flat. Keep moving.* You do move, *yes, I can,* but oh your feet feel so heavy.

You love Griffin, your mother's brother. He's your friend—you never thought to call him uncle. He heals stunned birds and crazy horses. If a neighbor breaks a wrist or ankle, Griffin Hayes will chop his firewood all winter. He'll stop to help any man or dog or child, but cannot save, will not lift his father. When you see Theo and Griff together, you want to hold them both, one in each arm, so that they can hold each other. Careful, these two—shake of the hand, grip of the shoulder—so afraid: don't touch too long, don't be too tender. You see how it is, how their minds hold them apart, how their bodies long to fall together. Why not fall? Why not let them?

Sometimes your cousin Tulanie falls out of his chair because he's drunk and stupid. He goes wheeling too fast, jumps the curb on purpose—still so dangerous, your cousin. You and Iris have to pick him up, right the chair, lift him to it. This is why: he loves his wounds, loves you and Iris to lift, to touch, to wash him. You understand how easily he could break a bone and not know it, how slowly Tulanie's cuts and bruises heal. Doctor Pierce has patiently described the particular risks of alcohol, why toxins fail to flush from Tulanie Rey's compromised body. *Compromised?* Tulanie says, laughing. One more lovely lie of language. Later he pounds his fists on his thighs, a flurry of brutal blows. You don't try to stop him. *Compromised?* He's weeping now. *I'm fucking indestructible.*

You remember climbing the brick wall of Emerson Elementary, you and Tulanie Rey, to get to the roof, nine years old, little monkeys. You couldn't do it now. The world has changed: the pull of gravity grown fierce, the spin of the earth too fast and powerful. But that day you were light and fearless, and you and Tulanie pissed off the roof together, great golden arcs, while the white winter sun lit you.

You whinnied and pranced, full of your miraculous selves, radiant, and the children in the schoolyard sang your names, and you were never coming down—nobody was ever going to touch you.

They did touch: the principal, your mothers—your kind, befuddled, strangely humiliated teacher—the firemen who finally came, who had to bring their ladder. Climbing up was good; climbing down impossible.

Your mother forbade you to see Tulanie Rey, a whole week apart, grief and torture. But Griffin came the third day, as if he knew, as if he'd sensed your sorrow. Somehow he charmed or mesmerized your mother. She let you go, and Griffin took you up his mountain. As you climbed, trees swayed in wind and watched you. Snow fell from their limbs—falling snow healed you into silence.

So it is, even now: when you go to Griffin, the lies of language stop, the need for words vanishes. Maybe you split some wood. Maybe you haul some water. You sit on his porch to clean your knives and oil them. Griffin sharpens the blades. He carves a crow; you whittle a whistle. The day opens. There is no end to it.

In late summer, he leads you along a path where he's left cedar masks in the woods, bear and owl, fox and coyote, high in trees, hidden in hollows. They are half alive, mouths open wide, eyes empty. He can't take the masks inside until the animals come and their spirits fill them.

The trail through trees opens to a high pasture where Joshua Troyer's two horses graze together. They stand one behind the other, facing opposite directions, lines of their bellies magically linked for a single moment. When they move, they are one being becoming two—a white Andalusian stallion and an elegant golden mare stepping gracefully into a green world.

Griffin saved the shimmering mare, taught her to eat again after she got into locoweed one summer. Now she presses her head to his chest to feel his heart and breathe him. He calls her

*Rika Marika, Little One, Darling.* He says she saved his life. He says, *We saved each other.* He slept in the pasture nine nights. She'd been eating Lambert's Crazyweed three weeks before Josh Troyer caught her. The starved mare was half-blind by then, knees locked, legs trembling. Her heart stuttered, and still she craved the weed and nothing else now that she had a taste for it. Marika's coat dulled to dust. Her sharp ribs rose, blades beneath thin flesh, bone knives slicing her. She'd die in another week if Griffin couldn't help her.

Griff says a rat will drop dead of a heart attack, high on cocaine, spinning in his wheel. He won't stop. He won't eat. If he's tired, he'll hit the bar for more coke and spin himself silly. Griffin's trying to tell you one of his own stories. He understands fear, what it means to be torn apart or snapped open, how important it is to wake and hear one sweet voice you remember. When he lies down with the little mare, he understands he can't heal her unless she lets him. They share their hunger. Marika drinks only water. *Three days,* Griffin says, *me too, and we were both clear and weak at the end of it, and she ate some hay, and we shared an apple, and Joshua and I hacked the crazyweed, but the poor bees had already lost their senses. They couldn't find their queen. They buzzed themselves sick and fell from the sky, hopeless.*

Rika knows Griffin loves her. She nickers from across the field and glides toward him, her gait so effortless and soft she seems to flow, the sheen of her golden self moving in and out of her body. She stops and waits, bends her long, beautiful neck shyly. She wants him to speak, not a word, just a murmur, *Rika, Marika,* her name a chant, a song between them. Only then does she dare to move close, stepping lightly into his shadow, into the air, the space between where she feels his body begin as warmth and vibration. He breathes as she breathes, and now at last, safe in shadow, she presses her head into his chest and shudders.

You wish Griffin and Theo could touch this way, here, under the blue blue sky high on Ruby Mountain where the curve of the earth becomes suddenly visible. Griffin does not fail to forgive: Theo fails to receive mercy. Pelle, the white horse, stands beneath a tree, camouflaged by limbs and leaves, a pattern of light fluttering across his body. The horse is the tree, and the tree is a shadow—the whole world hides here, close enough for you to touch it. You stroke Pelle's soft neck, and all the beings he ever was flood into you.

*Those with hope survive.* You don't have keys to jab in the ice. The house is unlocked. Why carry them? Your little knife is zipped in a tiny pocket near your ankle. Such clever pants, your favorite pair—eleven pockets in all, two inside, two invisible. Cold as you are, the one above your ankle is unreachable.

But it doesn't matter. There's no ice left to jab—you're free of that now. You've been sucked down and popped up a dozen times, bounced on boulders, snagged on wire, ripped clear and whelmed and swirled. Cold, yes, you were, you are, and it did hurt, but now it doesn't. You can fight or surrender. *Or float,* Griffin says. *It's only water.*

# 4

## Morning Twilight

Theo stands in Kai's tracks at the edge of the river, casts his blue beam over jagged ice, an open mouth full of black water. He wants to leap into the hole, let the river swirl him down and under, trust it to take him where he needs to be, wherever Kai is with Talia.

*Old fool.* They could be snagged on any root or rock. Even now the drenched boy might be dragging himself out, half frozen, staggering back along the riverbank to find him.

He calls, and waits. And calls—and waits.

The river roars under ice, churns dark in the hole Kai opened. Black limbs fracture brittle morning light, and he knows this is a sign: the boy will live, or the boy will vanish. The snow begins to glow, revealing every shattered crystal.

He calls once more, and this time the wakened owl hisses back in fury. What does he care for human sorrow? These woods are full of bones. When he takes flight, the dead rise up in his spectacular body.

A minute gone, a lifetime wasted.

Theo plants his flashlight in snow, the blue torch will be a place to begin—all he can do, next to nothing. He tries to run in his own footprints, follow them fast backward, but the holes are too far apart, old legs too weak and heavy. If he falls, he'll freeze, and no one will know how and why he finally failed. The rabid fox yips and follows. The dead are quick; they never leave you. His head throbs, vessels bursting. *Now, Theo.* He feels a man on fire, so close the cold air scorches him. *Would I have driven past or risked my life to save you?* He wants to turn and fight the fox, the flames, the icy river—go back and save himself, the burning man, his wife, his child.

Useless, this gasping body, *nothing to me*, sack of skin, bones rattling. He lurches forward, his only hope to reach the first house. *Now, before, so cold already.*

Lela wraps two sausages in a slice of bread. She can't wait. She'll eat in the car on the way to the hospital. Kai and Theo will find seven sausages still warm in the oven, eggs in the fridge stirred and ready to scramble, coffee in the pot, their favorite mugs, Naomi's flowering napkins. They'll know: *You, always.*

She meant to scold both son and father. Kai skipped school yesterday, twenty-seven absences since September, and Theo lied for the twenty-seventh time—he'd lie straight-faced to God for his grandson. *Let the boy have some freedom.* The high school counselor called Lela at work to ask what she knew. *It would be a shame*, he said, *if your son failed to graduate.* Was this a threat? She pictured the man: six-foot-four, blue eyes, blond buzz cut. *Perhaps there are extenuating circumstances.* Did Jared Donovan want her confession?

*I work two jobs because I failed to stay married. My son lives a secret life. I don't have time to follow him to school.*

Here's the truth: *He's seventeen; he's bored silly.* He wants to climb trees with his father, strap on a leather safety belt and daggered cleats and shimmy up pines with a chainsaw. Kai and Tim Dionne, tree trimmers extraordinaire—neither one understands the value of conjugating verbs in Spanish. They can't remember the years Stalin ruled or the day Czechoslovakia was invaded. They don't ever want to know how many Cambodians Pol Pot slaughtered. Neither father nor son can locate Moldova on a map of Eastern Europe or find Rwanda in the heart of Africa. But they can press their ears to the bark of a sick pine and hear beetles crawling. They hang like monkeys fifty feet above the ground, sawing dead limbs to save your precious house from summer fires. They're spidermen. They're wizards. If the wind kicks up, they ride it out, swaying in the tree tops. The saws they wield are quick and fierce: one kick can jolt you loose; one fast bite can break you. To reach the highest limbs, they carry long poles with handsaws. It's quiet work at the end of the day, two men restoring the world to silence.

Lela meant to talk to Tim too. She was glad about the job, the promise, father and son in business together. But she wants Kai to have that diploma. *A man can't climb trees forever.*

Last week, Tim stopped by the house to see Kai, and lingered in the kitchen alone with her after. Late afternoon light turned rose and coral. They spoke softly, and it wasn't the

33

words that mattered: it was the sound of their low voices intertwined that brought Kai down the stairs and into the coral light with them. Lela saw that her son's hands are bigger than Tim's, his shadow not as broad, but longer than his father's. She wanted to say it then, even before Jared Donovan's phone call, insist to both of them that if Kai meant to work with his dad, he had to finish high school. But the boy's shadow fell across the floor—his shadow touched her shoulder—and this touch was so strange and so familiar, so exquisitely tender, she laughed with the pure joy of it, and Tim laughed too, as if he saw, as if he knew exactly what had happened. It was their laughter in this light that made her believe if Tim stayed for dinner that night and returned every night for the rest of his life, it wouldn't seem wrong, and it wouldn't surprise her.

But he couldn't stay. Tim Dionne has another wife and two daughters waiting in another house fifteen miles down the road. He has a tree farm of perfect spruce growing in another world. *For when we're old*, he says to Kai, *all we'll have to do is plant and water*. He has a sloping yard where Kai spins his little sisters like airplanes, two flights of stairs where Juliana and Roxie ride their brother like a pony, up and down, a dozen times, till Kai falls flat on the floor and whispers, *You killed me*. The giggling girls fall down on top of him, kissing his neck, in love with their brother.

Later, they tie him to a chair with scarves and bandannas—they hide from him: one in the basement, one in the attic. How long will it take for Kai to come? The little girls can hardly stand it.

Lela imagines the life she doesn't share, the laughing girls who aren't her daughters. She let Tim go, that sweet night last week, and every night before it. And this too was good; this too was perfect. The father in her house is Theo. After dinner, Kai said, *I need your help, Grandpa.* They went to the cold garage where Kai is building a desk for his sister Juliana. Lela heard the buzz of the table saw as she cleared the dishes, the joyful syncopation of hammers drumming, a son's startled curse, a father's laughter. *I need your help, Grandpa.* This is all, and this is why, the mystery of an unseen plan: her child has restored her father.

Theo pounds at the red door, the first house on the road, lights upstairs and down blazing. He bangs the window with his head because his hands hurt too much to keep hammering. There she is, sweet savior, a woman on the other side of the glass, his double: dark hair, skin pale, scared of him, scared as he is.

She won't open the door.

He slumps against the window, *Please, my grandson.* She will not read his lips. She's got her cell phone now, is calling the police—*yes*, not to help, but to take him.

He remembers knocking on strangers' doors, the shame of it, looking for Griffin, his own son—Theo's runaway boy fourteen years old and wild. When he flew from his bedroom window, Griffin Hayes took only the clothes he wore, a three-ounce bar of bitter chocolate, a bag of dope, two hits of acid.

Was he hiding in the woods or a hundred miles gone by morning? Griffin loved slipping between worlds, diving deep in cold water, becoming the rainbow trout, proving how long he could stay under. The officer who took Theo's report said,

*He'll let you find him when he's ready.* Hours or days—years, depending. Theo Hayes tacked his son's picture to telephone poles, left him in grocery stores, taped him in windows.

One day, he saw a thin child tied to a fence post, sleeves of his windbreaker knotted behind his back like a straightjacket. He drove past because he didn't understand—he didn't believe it. By the time he circled back, the boy had slipped free and vanished, left only the red jacket as evidence, snagged on the fence, dangling to mock him. The jacket was far too small to fit Griffin, and still Theo understood, a sign: *You'll never catch me.*

The pale woman stands at her window, glaring out at him, and he's so cold he's gone silly. He points and laughs like a lunatic. He knows this is wrong—knows he's ridiculous—but he finds his howling reflection hilarious: he could die right here, even now, safe on this woman's porch, so close to mercy.

The call came eight months later, two a.m., the police in Missoula. *We've found your son, sir.* Griffin drunk or stoned. *Sleeping it off. No need to hurry.* Naomi wanted to go right then, that minute. *Drunk.* All this time, all this worry. *Let him piss in a pot. Maybe when he gets home he'll be grateful.* Your own child. Did you really say this? Theo's had thirty-seven years to repent, and he still can't believe he didn't pull on his pants and lace his boots and drive ninety miles an hour straight to him. All for a night's sleep. All to teach Griff a lesson.

Theo didn't sleep. He tossed, and Naomi lay awake beside him. At three minutes to three she said, *I'm gone, I'm going.*

The boy they retrieved was not their child. He'd lost nineteen pounds, five teeth, his right boot, his underwear, his jacket. Griffin Hayes had learned what he was willing to exchange for a night in bed or the promise of a meal. He'd scratched his flesh raw. *Never clean, so itchy—ticks and fleas, snakes and weasels.*

He wouldn't ride in front. *Even I smell me.* Naomi climbed in back to rock him. Griffin closed his eyes and tried to sleep, but woke two minutes later, twitching. He had a violet scar on his neck, an open wound down his belly. *Things happen when you dream. I saw a man downtown, frozen solid. Somebody slits your throat. Somebody sets your hair on fire. A boy cut off my ear one night, and a woman used her tongue to heal me.*

The police car turns the corner, thirty-seven years too late, no sirens wailing. The dark-haired little lady opens her door, teetering on her too high high heels, already sorry. The officers see him for what he is: an old man, perfectly harmless, no threat to them or the flustered woman who insists that just moments ago this human heap banged like a madman at her window.

One policeman squats beside him—just a boy, face rosy. *Can you stand? Are you injured?*

Theo's words slur, mind stupid.

The older man leans close to comprehend Theo's riddle. *The river, my child.*

This one has yellow skin, eyes too deep in his skull, children of his own, a life of sorrow. *Now*, he says, *this morning?*

*Yes.* Theo wants to weep, so grateful to the one who hears, the one who's come to save him.

He can't tell the officers how long it's been, can only say, *pink sky.*

Yes, that was the beginning, pink sky, mist of fog along the river opening.

The two men help him to his feet, and the young one says. *Do you know where? Can you show us?*

Theo nods, almost giddy with joy, head bobbing. *Yes, my flashlight.*

In the car, the flushed, sweet-faced boy calls for Search and Rescue. *Half an hour,* he says, *maybe forty minutes.* His voice is low, a man's voice rising out of a child's soft body.

*Forty minutes.* How can this be?

Theo can't believe the time since, that it is possible to measure.

PART TWO

# 5

## SILENT SNOW, SINGING SPARROW

3 FEBRUARY 2006: 10:00 A.M.

Daniel Sidoti knows he will be the one to find the boy and pull him from the river. He feels Kai's cold body inside his own, cold water running through them.

Hundreds have come to search. They carry ropes and blankets, knives and chocolate, thermoses full of hot broth or cider. They have slings to throw and harnesses to lift him. Daniel's knife will cut and strip, saw or puncture, dig a trench, snip wire. Thirteen firefighters tow a sled that glides on ice or floats on water. One wears a rescue suit, bright orange, with booties. *For walking on the moon,* he says. Or walking on the river.

Two hours gone. Ice heaves and cracks, fractures radiating from the jagged mouth of open water—a rumble now beneath ice, fissures widening. A pack of homeless kids with homeless dogs works the shore. *Those with hope survive.* The children know how dangerous it is to be wet, how quickly the senses go. They live by weird luck, wit, and will. *Nothing is impossible.*

41

Daniel is living proof of their belief. A boy in tattered camouflage waves as if he knows: Daniel Sidoti is one of them, the man who died, a walking miracle. Daniel survived nineteen hours after he swerved to miss the deer on Marias Pass—and did miss her—and spun on ice, and kept spinning. He rolled off the side of a cliff into a night of no degrees and absolute surrender. *Do you love only what returns love, or have you learned to love stone and silence?* The boy who waves has survived a hundred nights loving stars, naming snowflakes.

Daniel climbed with numb hands and fractured pelvis. He believed he would die before dawn. *But not right now, not in this moment.* He thought of his wife at home, his two little girls sleeping. Snow swirled. Nobody on earth knew he was missing. Seven mountain goats appeared on the hillside. He belonged to them tonight. He stayed alive in their eyes.

Daniel moves through these woods, quick and fearless. *Hope is the next breath, not the next hour.* Does God love silent snow less than singing sparrow? Daniel hears murmured prayers, wind through pines, *shushhh* of water. What is love? *Patient cloud, you inside me.*

So simply the day began: less than an hour ago, Daniel arrived at Tim Dionne's to tune Angie's piano. Only Angie was home—Tim's wife, but not Kai's mother. The boy visits twice a week, sometimes skips school to spend the day working with his father. This morning, as Angie braided Juliana's hair and helped Roxie find her favorite socks for school—as Tim warmed the truck and burned his mouth with coffee— nobody here imagined: Kai leaping after the dog he loves, ice broken on the river.

*Angie Dionne!* Proof of God, she is, for unbelievers. Daniel's heard her play, inventing music, as if she sees birds flung across a winter sky, swooping apart, rising, regathering—each bird, each note a part of all others, one cell in the great body of bird, wings and wind, clouds ringed with light, pure rapture. What man, what child could fail to love her? Daniel can't play, but he can hear—his father's curse, and blessing. He remembers the old man grown deaf, one hand on his chest and one on wood to feel the notes reverberate.

Daniel loves the peace of replacing strings and adjusting hammers, cleaning keys, restoring resonance. The perfect tone is not a single note, but harmonics resolving. This particular morning, he loved Angie there in the kitchen doorway, watching him work, protecting him from unseen harm, listening—listening. He remembers the light behind her, and Tim returning home unexpected—how surprised she was, how glad to see him—but he didn't close the door or stomp his boots, and a bright whirling wind poured through the house after him, and she knew before she knew, something strange and terrible, and all Tim said was *Kai, gone, the river,* and the coffee she cradled slipped through her hands and the cup shattered, and Daniel thought he heard the sound of light breaking through the kitchen window.

Now three women sing Kai's name across the water. *Is there a secret chord to call the scattered parts of you back into your body?* One calls to Talia, and the dog's name rings tree to tree down the river. *Talia! Hair frozen blue, heart beating wild—if Talia were alive she would bark you into being.*

Daniel calls in the voice of the owl, the *whoo – hoo* of one who has flown far, who has left his woods to creatures walking. *You—you must have seen, and might have followed. Now, if you choose to speak, you might return and take me to him.*

The night Daniel died he felt owls everywhere soaring above him, holding him in their precise gaze, feeling the heat of him, body against snow, hearing every gasp and whimper. So slow he was, crippled human! So small between earth and sky—no one, almost nothing. They could have torn him apart, but chose instead mice and rabbits. He began to know them as they knew him, to sense them even without seeing, to feel their weight above, the pressure of air against his back and thighs, rushing close, then receding. *Now you can die. Now you know everything.* Their lightness of being amazed him. The great gray came, and Daniel saw his blue shadow on snow, a bird three feet long, wings spanning sixty inches. *Imposter!* Hollow bone, fluff of feather, less than two pounds—curious enough to swoop down, but barely strong enough to lift a squirrel. *I will not take you off this mountain.*

Daniel saw his father limp in the bed, tangled in soiled sheets, half-blind, stone-deaf, terrified and wordless. The green vines of crumbling wallpaper tangled through the old man's skull as the tumor took one small gift and then another: a note, an eye, a pound of flesh, the sense of smell, the will to swallow. Daniel untangled the sheets, gently rolled the old man side to side—to change the damp bed, to wash him. *Such peace!* Afternoon light gold through gauze curtains. He lifted one frail leg and then the other, and washed between his father's legs, and washed one more time his father's hollow chest and shrunken buttocks. *Who can touch and not love? Who can be afraid to die, after?*

The old man watched him with his wild eye, amazed a son could be so tender. Was he cruel once, this helpless father? Did he shove the boy to the wall and cuff him? Did he take the rifle back as punishment for a crime so small they've both forgotten?

Downstairs, Daniel's sister Laurel and their mother Joy played violin and piano. The deaf man felt the sonata rising through the floor and tried to make a sound—a grunt, a gasp—to follow it. Daniel hummed the notes to calm him, lightly lifted his father's hand to his own chest, so the old man could feel it there, the last sound of the last day, resolving.

As Daniel spun on Marias Pass, as the world tilted into darkness, as tires lost their grip, and the truck began to roll, he was not afraid: the deer leaped free, alive in the living forest. *Everything goes on here, without us.*

So strange not to die, to unhook the seatbelt, to pull himself out through the shattered window, to hurt, to want to live, to crawl, to gasp, to breathe, to be so cold, to climb, to love your pitiful human life so much even now as you saw the end of it. *Does God love the grass frozen under snow less than the green blaze of summer?*

Daniel Sidoti climbed because there was more light at the rim of the cliff, a faint glow, moonlight on snow, and this seemed good, proof of something. He climbed because he saw seven mountain goats, white in the white world, below and then above, following or leading, curious and kind, black mouths always tender. Did they want him to climb? Did his life, his human heat, his heart matter?

He slept. Sleep was death. He knew it. Everything in the world was white: fox, stone, cloud, weasel. Soon enough snow would cover him. *When does one thing become another? How many seconds does the brain live after the lungs stop heaving?* Stars pierced the night. Daniel used all his strength to roll to his back and see them. *That which you call death has no meaning.* One mountain goat came close enough to touch. He smelled her, felt the warm nose, the heat of breath against his mouth as the animal breathed him. *Do you love your own mind? Are your human thoughts so precious?* He heard himself laugh. The other goats came, unafraid of him—nameless, helpless, half-human being.

He can't prove any of this is true, can't call owls and stars as witnesses. Only the spell of hypothermia, pain numbed by cold, brittle mind reeling with endorphins. That's what the doctors would say if he told them about the goats, how sweetly they loved him. The boy who waved—who gathered his shivering bones and tattered clothes from a heap of rags half buried in snow, who became human today by faith and will, *by love*, to search for one missing like himself—would believe every unspoken word of it. It is heat and hurt that give us the grief of hope and keep us clamoring.

*Sweet child lost, hiding in this river, do you cling to pain, or have you decided to live the rest of your days as light and shadow, the blue pattern of trees on snow, the green shattered on water?*

# 6

## River's Edge

Not yet noon and Iris McKenna thinks she's found her
cousin three times this morning.

He was a green garbage bag and red t-shirt, tangled in
roots, tugged by the current, half in and half out of the water.
Even when she understood, *nobody here*, she scrambled down
to the river's edge to tear the shirt free and watch the bag float
away from her.

Kai could be anywhere, wet on the shore or under the surface. Trapped beneath ice or pulled fast down an open channel. He'd leaped to save the dog—now both were gone, four
hours missing. Iris wanted to run, but was too cold and hungry, face numb, lungs aching. She stumbled between trees. *If
God is God, why can't I find him?*

A small mule deer watched from the woods. He smelled
human skin, the girl so close he could taste her breath in the
air between them. One leap shot him twenty feet away from

her. Branches snapped. *Why not you?* The animal blurred, flying out of himself. He bounded up the ridge, then stopped to look down on her. Snow fell from limbs he'd touched. *It might have been. It's still possible.*

The third time her cousin was a long-legged boy, loose in his stride, following the river, a child searching for himself, his own angel. He looked thin in the brittle light, as if the morning's struggle had already wasted him.

The quick boy was not easy to catch, and so fragile Iris was afraid the sound of his name might hurt him. He wore a black hooded sweatshirt beneath a cloth coat, a tattered camouflage of leaves stained dark by blood or oil. The child's naked hands looked raw, cracked by the cold, too big for his body.

When her shadow touched his back, the boy pulled down his hood and turned to face her. He was six inches shorter and thirty pounds lighter than Kai Dionne, his hair white blond and even finer than hers was. He had the face of a little fox, small and beautiful, delicate as a starved girl's, skin stretched tight, bruised green above the right eyebrow.

Iris remembered him as Peter Fleury. Now he's No, the name his friends use to tease and love him. *No* is his favorite word. He speaks no more words than necessary. He loves dirt and feathers, the woods at night, stars shattered. He sleeps in hollow trees, or digs a shallow grave and dies there. Snow is warm in its way, and quiet. He can't sleep in unlocked cars. *No, they smell like people.*

For luck, he wears his mother's sapphire ring on a cold chain around his neck, under his brother's too-tight t-shirt. He carries five baby teeth in a red silk pouch. *Where did I go?*

*Where are the others?* He'll pawn the ring if he ever gets that old or desperate.

*No, never.* Fifteen, he thinks, just last month, twelve days after Christmas—no bed, no walls three years now. He's lost eleven pounds and grown four inches. His bones speak. *Keep walking.* They pulse at night, spine to fibula, cells gone mad, multiplying and dissolving. He knows God this way. *The one who makes and unmakes me.* No's mother walked past him last week on North Pine and didn't stop because she didn't know him. Nadine Fleury came so close he smelled smoke and almost loved her. He could have snatched her purse. He could have killed her.

Two days later, he broke the basement window and slipped into her house to take the ring and his little brother's yellow t-shirt. He found his teeth rolled in a sock, tucked in a drawer, safe where he'd left them. He lay down in his mother's bed and pressed his face into her pillow. Would she know him if he died here? *No.* Thorns and rags, skull of a fox, brittle bones strung with sinew—just one more filthy thing to toss, a lost boy's broken puppet.

He left the seal of his hand on her mirror, fingers long and strange, palms lined with dirt and narrow. In another life, he'd pressed his little hand into white plaster, painted the imprint red and the smooth disk purple. She loved that hand, her favorite gift, Peter Fleury's seventh Christmas. Mother hung it on the kitchen wall, and there it stayed till No was nine and bad and broke it. *Is it true? Did he leap and grab? Did he throw it at her? Did he bite the hand that tried to stop him?* That's what she said. But No still believes he saw Mother rip it from the wall, and Peter Fleury try to save it.

He remembers plaster smashed on kitchen tiles, the white inside exposed, the red and purple shattered. Little brother Nick stood in the kitchen doorway, clutching his sock monkey. The creature grinned his terrible orange grin. He loved grief—yes, just what he expected.

No remembers himself on his knees, trying to make the pieces fit, trying to push them back together. His face buzzed. How many times did she hit? How hard did she do it?

Mother was somewhere else now, suddenly gone, then Nick and the monkey vanished too, and Peter was alone in the light on the floor, so maybe he made it up, or maybe he dreamed it. Maybe he cut his fingers on the broken hand. Maybe he bit them.

He bites them now. Iris pulls off her gloves and holds them toward him. No, he won't—she's colder than he is. Snow whirls up from the ground between them. They never speak. What would they say here? *Beautiful, the snow is.* He spins and leaps. *The disappeared can't wait.* Ice cracks along the river.

He's not trying to lose her. She can follow if she wants. She won't hurt him. *Heart, skin, breath, believer.* She could make him whole today. They might find the missing boy, and bring him home alive together.

# 7

## Niña, Pérdida
### *Love Song for Iris*

Forty-seven days before she was born, Iris McKenna kicked you in the head hard enough to jolt you. Fierce, your Iris. Aunt Christine lay sprawled on the bed, flushed despite the cold day, sweat beading on her lip, belly strangely tight and swollen. You and Tulanie brought cool rags to wash her. She wanted you to touch, *here and here*, behind her knees, between her fingers. She pulled you close. *Don't be afraid. Say hello to your cousin Iris.*

You were only four, but you'd already seen unborn sparrows, the nest torn from a tree, three turquoise eggs cracked open. The pitiful creatures inside might have become birds or lizards. You'd seen a calf emerge from his groaning mother—a slick, limp-legged animal that fell to the grass, dark and bloody. His mother licked him to life—and as you watched, you felt it: wet tongue, cool grass, your trembling naked self, *don't be afraid*, life on earth, in the beginning.

You pressed your little hands and then your ear to Christine's hard stomach, and Iris, who swears to this day she remembers, squirmed and jabbed and finally nailed you. Tears welled—not from pain, but from the sharp surprise of it. Christine said, *This little girl will give you trouble.*

She did and she does: Iris Jenae, Queen of the Skate Park, Queen of the Mountain, thirteen just last week and dangerous to you in ways Tulanie never was. She'll fly you off a cliff if you follow her on your snowboard. You can't scare Iris. *Nothing to lose.* Her mother's gone, her brother broken. *I'll start an avalanche someday and wake up buried.* You see a cave of snow, a womb, a cradle—Iris not dead for days or hours.

Last summer, twelve-year-old Iris led you down a ravine and through a culvert. Somewhere in the dark tunnel under the road, your quick little cousin turned herself inside out and lost you on purpose. You sensed her all day. In the woods she was smell of pine and damp earth, bones of a bird, wing and feathers—at the river, Iris: cold water against your skin, smooth stone, one limb thick with leaves floating past you.

Late that night she called you on your cell phone. *I waited,* she said. *Where were you?* A trick, a game—Iris in love; Iris, your lover. *Niña Pérdida.* Iris McKenna five years old and lost: this little girl will never forgive you.

You and Tulanie were not quite ten, big boys set free on a summer day, your mother at work, Christine sleeping. Your aunt had been at the hospital all night, taking care of other people's children. Night nurse, angel—she's not afraid to touch the sallow, bloated boy whose kidneys have failed him. She loves the night, cradle of darkness. She rocks the baby with blistered feet, scalded in her bathwater. Last winter she saw a boy with every bone in his face shattered. That one hit a tree, sailing on his snowboard. Now there's the girl stung thirty times, the boy whose flesh is peeling. No wonder she's plunged, drowned in the drugged sleep of day, head thick with heat, whole body buzzing.

*I need you,* Christine said, *to watch out for Iris.*

In your cousins' backyard bright with dandelions, Tulanie shot you with his BB gun, and the pellet grazed your temple. One inch to the right would have pierced your eye and gone straight through you. You whooped and reeled, dizzy with the thrill of it. Iris yelped too, and you held her high to spin and twirl, danced her to the end of the yard and round and round in circles. *Iris.*

Giant poppies blazed at the side of the house, crimson and orange, white and scarlet. You knew how to pluck the blossoms from their stalks, flip them upside down, and turn them into ballerinas: their heads the tiny pods, their flaming skirts the fragile petals. You looped and spun till poppies flared, a ring of fire around you. You remember that sweet-little-girl-dirty-Iris smell: milk and mud, grass and bananas—arms tight around your neck, skin soft as torn petals. Tulanie shot you again with his fingers, and you fell down dead in the tall grass, and little Iris fell on top of you.

What is love if not the weight of one so familiar?

You left Iris in the yard and told her not to follow. Tulanie said, *Wake Mom when you're hungry.* You sped away on your mountain bikes. *I need you,* Christine said, *so tired. Yes,* you understood. *Yes,* you promised. You tried not to look back, but

you knew—you saw her: Iris pedaling hard on her pink tricycle—so small, so far behind—Iris following the boys she
loved, Iris trying to catch you.

How long is a day in the life of a child?

You climbed the cliffs below Lone Pine. Tulanie scrambled
fast, twenty feet above you. One stone pulled loose in his grip
and you saw it drop but couldn't dodge it. The sharp edge
struck your brow. Fingers blurred; you couldn't feel them. Did
you close your eyes? Clouds and sky appeared in negative.
The pellet in the backyard was Tulanie's warning shot: this
was the place where your cousin would kill you. Torn poppies bloomed in your skull, red into red, black at the center.
Your fingers slipped and you let go. Nothing hurt. Nothing
scared you. You held your breath. What could you do but fall
backward? Then the whole sky turned blue, dark blue, and a
hawk whirled high, your only witness. You smelled milk and
mud, skin on skin, Iris here, all around you. Something tender
pushed you back. A rush of wind? You felt so light, so numb,
so much like air itself, you still believe this is possible.

At the river hours later, Tulanie tied a rope high in a tree,
and you flung yourselves to deep water. You loved the cold,
the dark current, your body gone, swept down and under. You
couldn't die. You were nothing now, nothing but the green
shadow of yourself swimming on the bottom.

You lay on hot rocks in hot sun and felt the bones of yourself bleached and scattered. A brilliant tanager swooped tree
to tree, gold and orange, black-winged, silent. You were what
you saw, and your quivering body rose, flying with him.

Tulanie leaned close to whisper. *I thought you fell. I thought I
saw you.*

When you rode home between the trembling shadows of trees, you were little boys again, hungry and cold, children alone, missing your mothers. Aunt Christine ran into the road to greet you, and Tulanie swerved, but his father snagged him. Christine slapped and clutched, and slapped and kissed him. Your mother appeared in their doorway, and you knew why and what you had done even before Uncle Roy said it.

Iris gone, all this time.

*Where were you?*

You remembered the last time you turned to look. Your cousin's sandals blinked off and on, red and blue, lights flashing. Iris sparkling in the sun, Iris twinkling as she pedaled. You'd had sneakers with lights—once upon a time, just last year or the year before—when you were very small, when you were still a child, slight and fair, but not ever as quick to burn, as thin, as breakable as Iris. You missed those shoes. You missed the little boy long lost who'd worn them. That child loved his Batman mask and black pajamas. He fell asleep on the couch, and his mother scooped him up and carried him to his bedroom. So light! So clean! You, yourself, imagine. Your mother who loved you lifted the mask to kiss your cheeks and eyelids. If you lay very still, she might lie down and sleep and stay here. She traced the shape of your face. *I know who you are. My fingers see you.* She was yours, all yours, forever yours, since your father left you. Your mother's cool fingers smelled of crushed mint and lavender. She sang as trees sing, so softly the words were not words, but another breath inside you. Stars sparked between the dark leaves of the maple, and you wanted to stay awake all night, but sleep came as love to steal you.

Never now. You're too mean or too old. You come home too dirty. *Filthy*, your mother says, but she won't take a bath with you tonight, or any night—won't ever again make her body a raft to float you.

Later you remembered other things: Iris in the middle of the street, Iris at the corner near the school—a child wavering in the heat, a body turning into water. You remembered five braids in her blonde hair, each tied with a different colored ribbon. When you fell down in the grass, you held her head against your chest and breathed her. *Niña Pérdida*. Iris wearing blue shorts with white stars. *Little Girl Lost*. You saw signs tacked to trees, your cousin described in English and Spanish. You loved those shorts. Just last week Iris pulled you into her closet and shut the door to show you how stars glowed without the lights on. *That's how I find myself under the bed or under the covers.* You remembered the tiny top she wore, bright yellow, a halter tied in a double bow at the neck and a tight triple knot in back so she wouldn't undo it. Iris liked to be bare. Iris loved to be naked. She was always losing her clothes, coming home in muddy underpants and twinkling sandals.

You remembered her naked arms and bare belly, pink in the bright light, Iris already sunburned. *Niña Pérdida*. Eight p.m., eight hours gone, you and Tulanie Rey to blame for it. You thought they'd find her in the night, stars on her shorts and lights on her sandals flickering, but then it was the next day, and your little girl lost stayed lost.

The police questioned you three different times, three different men: red-faced and stooped, slack-bellied and tender—all with sad, serious eyes, all with guns strapped in their holsters. The third one looked squeezed into his uniform, muscles hard in his thighs, thick in his chest bulging. Officer Kite, Brian Kite, you remember. He put his arm around your mother before he left, kissed her almost on the mouth when he thought you couldn't see them. You had no right, no power to stop this. You said the same thing over and over: *Corner of Seventh and Fifth last time I saw her*. The policemen made you describe braids and stars, sandals and ribbons. Dark-skinned Brian Kite made you cry with all this Iris remembering. *We'll find her*, he said to your mother, and then the kiss, and the big hand on her pale arm lingering. Who was this man, and how many times before today had he kissed her?

Iris Jenae McKenna, five-and-a-half years old, forty-two inches high, thirty-nine pounds dripping. She could be any-where: down a ditch, in a culvert, curled up small as a cat, safe in her own closet. She had a doll almost as big as she was. Natasha sat on the bed, smiling as if she knew, as if she loved her secret. The clever doll had no string to pull to make her talk, no tongue to twist, no voice box.

After you and Tulanie rode away, Iris crawled into the narrow space under Thom Kizer's porch, just three blocks from the corner where heat rising off cement made the sun-scorched girl on the tricycle shimmer. Iris wanted to hide—to pay you back, to trick you. She tugged at the bow of her halter till it came loose and she could slip free of it. Your cousin left her shirt under the porch, *because*, she said, *it itched me*. Seven hours later, Thom's scrappy little black crossbreed discovered the cloth and dragged it out to show her people. Lulu had a sheep-dog's love for finding the lost, a terrier's will to hang onto it.

Thom had to tug and tear. He was afraid to take the tiny shirt inside, afraid to show his wife Elsa. Yesterday, they'd seen a sonogram of their child swimming in the womb—peaceful, she was, miraculously silent. She had a name they wouldn't speak. *Not till she's safe here.* Now this, a yellow flag—proof: *Anything can happen.* He stood on the porch, twisting the rag while Lulu leaped and yipped, thinking the man she loved would give it back if only she jumped higher.

Iris expected you and Tulanie to come begging, scared now, voices breaking—but you didn't come, so she scooched out from under the porch, hands and knees and belly filthy. A bent nail ripped her shorts. Iris knew there'd be trouble.

Two p.m., two hours gone, not yet missed or officially missing, Iris Jenae McKenna stopped to wash herself by running through Dwight Halliday's sprinkler. *I tried to help, but she ran away. I swear she had two big boys with her.* A lie. Iris alone, he knew it. Dwight Halliday opened his window and yelled. *You—get away from there.* He hobbled outside to give her a swat, but his left leg dragged, heavy in its brace and withered. All the children mocked him. What did they know about a hospital far from home, cribs with metal bars, a cast from neck to toe, an iron lung, a prison? He stood up and fell down, learning to walk again, after. Four years, and then his mother died, as if his pain had killed her. *Scarecrow,* the children said. *Scarecrow,* they still called him.

The nasty, half-naked little girl stuck out her pink tongue and tried to bite him. She was slippery and quick. He couldn't hang onto her. He had two of his own, a boy and a girl, but they never called, not once, after their mother abandoned him. Where the scarecrow gripped, four bruises bloomed on Iris McKenna's soft arm. If anybody asked, she could prove Dwight Halliday was the one, *the only one who hurt me.*

Now the torn shorts were soaked and not clean at all, but muddy. The day was hot, but she was cold, too tired to ride, so she stashed the pink tricycle behind a box in Arlo Dean's open garage and started walking. Six hours later, Arlo revved up the old Chevy and caught a glitter of pink in the beam of his headlights. He'd seen pictures on the news, the girl's mother weeping. He wanted to throw the tricycle in the bed of the truck and head to the dump and be done with it. Arlo Dean, twenty-three years old, four months out of prison. He'd met Roy McKenna there, a big man, like his father. Now Arlo was home again, living in his mother's basement, trying to stay straight, working night shift at a bakery. Why this? He'd be suspect and savior, the one who might confess, the one to lead them to her. He left the truck rumbling in the driveway— the sound of it, the yellow lights, gave him strange peace, time outside of time, a path to walk, a moment's comfort.

*I'll take him apart,* Uncle Roy said, *rip out his spine if he's got her.* He remembered Arlo from his time in Deer Lodge, a skinny, black-haired kid lucky to survive a single week in prison. Arlo Dean—pierced eyebrow, pierced nipples—no rings allowed in lock-up, but Roy had seen the holes when Mick Withers and Felix Joyce pinned him in the shower. The pale boy had scars running up his arms, scars on his thighs and stomach— not from them, but from long ago, his own knives and razors. So easy to die—blink of a blind eye, and the body opens—in the bathtub at home, in the shower of a prison. Arlo ran away at sixteen, lived in his truck to finish high school—not a bad kid, not really—but Arlo Dean walked home one cold, wild night and shot his father in the belly.

*He might have bled to death if he'd been human.* Arlo said, *I just wanted to be warm that night, but the door was locked, and I pounded hard, and I said, Come out, and he did, and my fingers hurt, and I shot him.*

Vernon Dean was dead, not from his son's wounds, but from a heart attack ten months later.

*Rip out his spine.* You looked at your uncle's hands. You'd seen him tear down walls and torch a trash heap, gut a doe and drown a packrat. He's the Disaster Man, the one who comes after flood or fire. He rolls up the blood-stained carpet, fixes holes in the attic roof, catches squirrels and bats to free them. He'll haul half a house away, then tenderly rebuild it. If Uncle Roy decides to take a man apart tonight, he'll do it.

In late afternoon, long before Arlo discovered the tricycle stashed in his garage, little Iris stood in Violet Kinshella's yard, eating ripe raspberries by the fistful. One sandal still blinked when she moved, but the other had flickered out, soaked by the sprinkler. She wiped her hands on the ripped shorts, and the stars almost disappeared, streaked dirty red, juice and mud mixing.

Violet sat at the kitchen window, but never truly saw the child. She had no vision left at the center, only the edges of sight where trees walked in wind and clouds fell from the sky like angels. Iris was one of them, trick of light or hungry ghost, Violet's long-lost little sister. *Clarita!* Why was Violet the one to outlive all the others? Born blue and never married, face scarred by pox, legs bowed by rickets. God spoke in a father's voice: *My little one, my sparrow*. He stole the last kiss and blurred the memory of faces. Three sisters, seven brothers lost, gone—all the way over. God offered the consolation of color: blue and green, rose and lavender—the pure apprehension of things, swirling sky, sun on water. God spilled merciful laughter: children in the street, loon and chickadee, bobolink, warbler. The little sister shape by the raspberry bush skittered and vanished. Clarita said, *Don't be sad. I'll come back someday to get you.*

Next door, Iris dropped her sticky shorts in Kira Champeaux's plastic wading pool. Kira's brother found the soaked rag less than an hour later, stuffed the evidence in the trash, never told his mother Roslyn. Why risk blame? Davi Champeaux had enough trouble, fourteen years old and already under house arrest, shackled to a monitor. He stole his father's car in June, brought it home crumpled. Today, the boy was too buzzed to worry, mellow on his mother's Vicodin, three or four, so limp now he can't remember. What did his father care about the crushed car? Daryl Champeaux had a new wife with red hair, a glossy black truck, a burbling baby daughter. Davi sprawled naked in the shallow pool, right leg dangling over the side so he wouldn't flood his beeper.

At dusk, Iris McKenna heard voices singing her name. She couldn't go home, clothes lost and torn, belly burned, legs so dirty. She pulled a white sheet from Miriam Gill's clothesline and climbed the ladder to Shoshanna's tree house. She wanted that little girl's life tonight: giant polar bear, plush panda—she saw the pretty gold room lit below her—green quilt with a hundred birds, music box with twirling dancers. She wanted to be home and not home, safe in another bed, loved as a different child.

*Iris, come out.* The voices scared her. *Don't take rides. Don't even smile at strangers.* She heard her mother's voice, high and brittle, and the strange, familiar sound scared her more than any other. Night poured through the slats and window. Night filled her secret house, and the leaves said, *Iris, Iris,* softly without need, softly without anger. A dog howled—or maybe a coyote. Then all the dogs cried out, barking back, whimpering. Terrified voices trying to sound kind said, *Iris, where are you?* Her mother's voice drifted beyond reach; her mother walked in the wrong direction. Darkness surged. *Hush, now, little one, no one's going to hurt you.* She loved the black wave rocking her. Everything in the world sang: owls and frogs, goats and crickets. One delirious cat shrieked, *Iris.* And then the night came fast. The night drowned her.

She woke too cold to sleep even with the sheet wrapped three times tight around her. Soft rain fell almost silent in the grass. Rain pattered on roofs far away and rolled down slanted wood right above her. Rain splashed in the street, rushed in rivulets along the gutters. Rain began to leak and drip and fall on her inside the tree house.

She'd slept hard on her left foot and now it flopped, numb and prickly. She remembered Tulanie stealing her shoe in the grocery store, a day long ago, when she was so tiny. Her bad brother stuffed the shoe in a freezer along the aisle, then put it back on her foot, all without their mother seeing. Iris bellowed so hard her insides quivered. The sound hurt and felt good until her mother smacked her. She thought of him now, Tulanie holding her shoe, Tulanie riding away from her. Her foot tingled back to life. If she ever got home again, she'd pull on her white cowgirl boots and use the heels to stomp her brother's bare feet, the sharp toes to kick him.

She had to walk or freeze, so she slid down the ladder, dragging the damp sheet behind her. Before it knows rain, does the poppy know sorrow? Iris cried in the rain, and the cool rain streaked her. Iris McKenna, fifteen hours lost, would have climbed in any car, and gone home with any stranger.

Then she was safe, near her own street, and she knew it. She heard Dugan howling from his dog house. Dugan, her friend! His head was huge and kind, square and funny. All of him was huge, black and gold, hair wiry. Dugan didn't scare her. Last winter, when she was so much smaller than she was now, she gave the dog half her peanut butter and banana sandwich. He swallowed it in one gulp, then stuck his nose through the fence to lick her face and fingers. Now, whenever he catches her scent, when he finally sees her, Dugan lopes to the high chainlink fence, barking and prancing. He tries to climb the fence, tries to squeeze his big boy self through the tiny spaces to get to her, his little love, his secret.

But tonight, Dugan doesn't smell Iris in the rain, doesn't hear her footsteps. He's hiding in his house and can't see the ghost girl wrapped in a sheet walking toward him. He's busy with his own grief, worn out from whimpering. She has to say his name twice before the yowling becomes a joyful yip, and then a long, lonesome cry, a human plea: *Come inside, come faster.* She finds a place where Dugan has dug deep at the edge of the yard, planning his escape, digging a tunnel.

She leaves the wet sheet crumpled on the sidewalk and scrambles under the fence. Never never in her whole dirty life has Iris McKenna been this dirty. She crawls into Dugan's house, curls inside his soft dog bed, presses her shivering self close as she can against his warm dog body. He's the only being on earth tonight, the only one to love in the whole wet world.

In morning light, into a day brilliant after rain, child and dog emerged together. Never before had the grass been so green. Never had so many birds sung from so many distances: thrush and wren, flicker, vireo. Never had the sky been so blue—never again so blue after. Floyd Lillie called to Dugan, and the big dog came to the back door, side by side with the tiny child. Every day surprised Floyd: Beatrix gone since last November—and still the sunflowers grew eight feet tall, and still the crows pecked them—stab of thorns, smell of roses— everything here but her; everything so beautiful. His wife waited in the urn on the mantel. Sixty-one years they'd been together. He had a house full of photographs, three daughters gone and grown, little girls lost and married. Only the dog knew his thoughts. Only the dog's tongue touched him. Every night he prayed: *Please, Lord, I'm ready.*

And now, today, here she was, the child lost come back to save him. God crushed him to reveal his purpose. *I need you to watch out for Iris.* Floyd washed her at the kitchen sink: arms and legs, mud-streaked belly. Beatrix showed him the purple bruises on her soft arm. *Don't ask. Be careful.* Never had he known more shame or gratitude. He wrapped her in his flannel shirt. Was she afraid? *No, hungry.* He fed her bread with jam, warm milk with honey. Beatrix stayed close—not to help, but to witness. *Yes, love, here is your answer.*

All those minutes before he called, before the policeman came with the child's mother and father, Iris was his, the way his three daughters were his, and Floyd Lillie was himself, called back to life, his own life, life on earth, in the beginning.

Last summer, when Iris slipped free of you in the dark dark of the black culvert, you whispered, *Please. Don't leave me.* But the little girl was long gone and never heard you. Tears stung. If you hadn't already been blind in the dark, your hot tears would have blinded you. You cried out her name three times, and each time cool cement roared *Iris* back at you. Everything you believed broke away in a single moment. You loved Iris— she completed you. Iris Jenae McKenna, twelve years old, your own cousin. The impossible pain of it brought you to your knees and you crawled through the slick black water of the culvert sobbing. When you emerged in the terrible light, you sensed her everywhere: Iris behind every tree, Iris stalking you. You staggered through the woods, tears staining your cheeks—so ashamed, so unable to stop them. You pressed your face to white birch and stumbled on the roots of cedar.

She must have known. She must have seen you. Everywhere you walked you left the bodies of crushed flowers.

You lay awake half the night, hand on your phone, under the pillow. She finally called. *I waited*, she said. *Where were you?*

She's waiting now. She wants to save you. She's blue, here, right beside you—sweet blue shadow of a spruce rippling on the water. If you can grab one limb and then another, you might pull yourself to shore and rest and breathe, and not die, not yet, not in this moment. You might tear your hands on stone and touch one more time smooth skin of weeping willow.

# 8

## A Song Unbroken

Five crows perch in a single tree, weirdly silent. *What is there to say?* The drowned dog rises and sinks with the pull of the water. She's trapped between ice and stone—snagged but not saved by a coil of wire. *Is it wrong to love her?* She's beautiful still, silky blue in the shadows. Arlo Dean crouches at the river's edge. *Everything dies.* The bank's too steep for him to reach her. One crow swoops low, and the choir starts squalling.

The clever birds could free Talia, tug and twist the barbs of wire. One day Arlo watched a crow pull a pin from a gate to chase nine rottweilers across a field. The dogs yelped, and the crow shrieked, wild with laughter. Later, a whole congregation appeared to feast on dog food. Such joyful noise, their blistering racket.

These five squawk and crackle, waiting for Arlo to understand, to drag Talia out and open her. *Life for Life—isn't hunger the blessing?* Arlo watched crows rise as he left work that morning, fifty or a hundred then, flapping hard, yammering. The sky glowed between their wings. *But you didn't believe. You didn't trust us.*

Eight years out of prison, and Arlo Dean is still amazed he's free to follow birds, or go home and crash in his mother's basement. He stopped for coffee—extra large, extra dark, six packets of raw brown sugar.

For small gifts, he's grateful: every morning of his life Arlo Dean can choose to do this. He's free to work alone, in peace, night shift at the bakery—no one watching his skinny back, nothing to hear but bread rising.

He figures he drank 2,088 tepid cups of pale coffee down in Deer Lodge. Hot water was dangerous—tempting, it's true: Arlo wanted to blind the ones who peered into his cell or gawked in the shower. He was never not seen, never not visible.

He received one teaspoon of white sugar each day, which he could use to sweeten the pitiful coffee or sprinkle on his glob of oatmeal. Exchanges were possible. If he managed to hoard or steal six aspirin, if he cleaned another man's cell, or knelt on the floor to cut that man's gnarled toenails with contraband clippers, Arlo might score an extra teaspoon for Easter.

If he'd had the patience to count the white grains, that number would equal his humiliations exactly. When his mother said, *Do you need anything?*, the only word in his mind was *sugar*.

She bleached her hair blonde after his father died, and here she was, so strangely radiant. *Beautiful*, he said, *like Marilyn*. She laughed in her lovely rippling way, three rising notes, and then a soft falling flutter. The other men in the visiting room turned to see her. Beautiful, yes: it was almost true, true enough from a distance—Marilyn Monroe grown thin and tired, lipstick glossy pink, bright hair a halo. Light from high windows caught the fine strands and sizzled.

He was allowed to hold his mother's hand, but not allowed to let his knees touch hers under the table. She bought them each a bag of popcorn, and he tried to eat, to please her, but his throat hurt, and he couldn't swallow.

One night they killed a man in the single-wide trailer just outside the prison wire—lethal, legal, injection for murder. His fingers curled for the last time—*Sleep now, Little One*—twelve witnesses watching—*Life for Life*—so close they smelled each other's heat, breath and skin, damp leaves burning.

*Do you need anything?*

Arlo's mother was permitted to kiss his cheek, to leave a shimmering pink imprint, to hold her son in her arms while the guard's watch ticked away thirty seconds.

*Ten seconds more. Touch me.*

Arlo was the prison gardener, trusted with a tiny spade, a trowel, a metal claw for digging. He wanted to tell his mother how perfect the tulips were, how much he loved them. He'd done nothing to deserve this: the tulips bloomed because they bloomed—they couldn't stop themselves from opening. They were soft rose or deep violet—scarlet, orange, peach, ruby—white inside or streaked with yellow. *Do you know my voice?* He felt them listening.

They had magical names: Queen of the Night, Blushing Beauty. They were Golden Surprise and Pale Fire. One morning it snowed, and he thought they'd die, but he knelt to scoop the ice from each blossom, murmuring as he touched, *be well, be healed*, and the sun pierced the clouds, and the rays of light saved them.

*Why all this talk of God?* The dog shattered ice, and the boy leaped after her. *You might have saved them both—if only you'd come faster.* The crows couldn't wait for Arlo this morning, but he found these five again, hungry at the river—and the sun rose, and the coffee was sweet and hot and bitter—every day, every breath, these miracles. Where water flowed free of ice, light slanting through trees streaked the river gold and silver.

No wonder the crows mock him now. They can mourn like doves, but prefer this jackling. Six hours gone. Two crows swoop so close he thinks they'll take him.

He sees Iris McKenna on the opposite shore. He'd recognize her any day of her life, from any distance, *Iris*, forever his since the day she stashed her pink tricycle in his garage and vanished. *As if you knew, as if you chose me.* Eight years since that day—perfect, he was, four months out of prison, a weird pale man living in his mother's basement: *Arlo Dean, Person of Interest.*

The police questioned him for two hours. *Help us*, they said. *We just want to find her.* Iris McKenna, five years old and so small—*thirty-nine pounds*—a hundred pounds lighter than he was—blonde, sunburned, *Iris*, blue shorts with white stars: *I'm sure you remember.* The officers showed him pictures of the little girl lost until he wanted to confess, until he loved her.

*Rip out his spine.*

He's still afraid of her father, those words, Roy McKenna's long fingers, the way he can't stop feeling them, imagining himself, a silvery fish sliced down its back, still alive, all his bones in one clean pull lightly lifted out of him.

If he passes Roy McKenna in the parking lot, if they move toward each other down the long aisle of a grocery store, they pretend not to see, not to know, not to remember that night, the words, the rain, the terrible sorrow—they look up and nod at the last possible moment, so polite, almost shy, like boys, both embarrassed, two men who met once upon a time long ago in prison.

He thought he'd die if she died. He lay on his bed in his basement room, watching the news at midnight. *Now, tell me.* He tried not to look for the little girl because he didn't want to be the first to see—wherever she was, whatever had happened. But the rain came, and a cold wind blew through the open window, and his skin hurt, *Iris,* and he walked out in the rain, and came home in the rain without her.

*Is this love?*

She didn't die. She spared him.

Today, her cousin is the child lost, and Iris hopes to find him. Hundreds have come to search. In the beginning, they sang the boy's name, full of hope, voices brilliant. Now, their footsteps are their prayers, the wind their breath, a word inside them. They've scattered far along the river's edge, each one alone, borne by faith or fear, finding a path moment by moment.

*Do the crows understand love?* He's heard them laugh with loons and churr to vireos. One sweet day when he was small and quiet, he found a family of crows lying in a field, wings spread wide, eyes half-closed as if they'd all swallowed poison.

But it was only the sun, warm grass, the bliss of being crows after so much clamoring. They spoke in secret trills and warbling whistles. Later, they chased a hawk into the woods, their cries harsh as his, clear and cruel.

He could call to Iris, but he lets her go, lets her believe in Kai and Talia. She's following a boy in tattered camouflage, skittery and quick, moving in and out of shadow. He's one of the starved children who waits for Arlo at the back door of the bakery, hoping for misshapen loaves and day-old pastries. The crows come too, day after day, hungry angels. *You think it's easy eating half your weight in garbage?* Sometimes Arlo slips the kids warm cinnamon rolls straight from the oven, a plastic knife, a slab of butter. He gives them five dollars for milk, and they laugh. *As if,* Neville says. They never thank him.

One dark December morning, Rikki said, *You can have me—a dollar a minute.* She's twelve years old. *Almost a virgin.* Crows count crimes generation to generation. If your grandfather blasted birds, their children's children find you.

He's passed a dozen homeless kids today—*Trina, No, Neville, Rikki*—and he wants to tell them all to go home—*if it's not too late, if it's still possible.*

Ridiculous now, the fights with his father. *You can't argue with the dead. They besiege you with memory.* There was the day Vernon Dean threatened to burn his black jeans and ripped T-shirt. *No need,* Arlo said, and did the job for him—stuffed his own clothes with straw, set his bad self on fire. He left the earth scorched, for this he was sorry.

Another day, not so long after, Arlo found Mother in his basement room, feeling inside his shoes, shaking his pillows. *Oh, sweet Lucie*—so sad to see her, the one he loved, the one who didn't scare him—Mother crawling under his bed, Mother in his closet weeping.

She confiscated four knives and a carton of Kools, a precious blue bottle full of Darvocet and Oxycontin, discovered one lucky day in Darla Fiori's dresser. That patient girl had stolen the pills one by one from her suffering parents. Arlo's mother snatched the nasty speed he'd scored from Jackson Toller—ten fat, black capsules, a vile high, cut with baby laxative and strychnine. Arlo dropped three hits one night and shit himself silly, muscles frozen hard, little heart shrinking. But he kept the stuff stashed—*in case of emergency*.

Lucie Dean repossessed thirteen cans of cat food, meaning she didn't want him to feed raccoons at his windowsill. She left the razor blades because she didn't know how he opened the skin of his arms and legs in her bathtub, carving a jagged heart in his thigh, etching a stick man in his belly.

*Grounded*, his father said, *three months, no privileges*. He demanded the keys to Arlo's truck, white with a blue door and green fender, the beautiful battered truck he'd salvaged from the junkyard.

Crazy now to think of it, choosing between his mother and the truck, his bed and the car seat. Sometimes sweet-skinned Emily Boone let him shower at her house, and he took whatever he found, whatever he needed: her father's flannel shirt, the gun from her mother's nightstand.

Once, just once, sweet Emily stepped into the shower with him, and they kissed until the water ran so cold it pierced them.

He was proud of himself, living in the truck, not flunking high school. He worked three nights a week at 7-11, and those nights he got dinner—a burrito or corn dog—barely chewed, quickly swallowed. Emily said, *I'd fall for you if you weren't so skinny.*

The little gun was his best friend, small enough to tuck down his pants, heavy enough to cock him off balance. He needed the pistol at work because you never knew when some hopped-up kid low on cash might take you down for a liter of Coke or an ice cream sandwich.

Then it was Christmas, reindeer leaping over roofs, lights everywhere twinkling. In the park, deep snow crusted hard on benches, melted and froze—*yes, here, lost children buried.* A thousand crows flocked together, their bodies becoming one for the night—this body warm, this voice silent. He saw seven drunken Santas leaving a bar together, red suits stuffed fat, fat cheeks all rosy. They tugged each other's beards and punched each other's bellies. One fell down, and the others howled, piling on top of him.

The day after was worse, and the day after that, his birthday. The merry lights blinked on and on, but everything was over.

A clear night, stars splintering, terrible and cold, so the birthday boy tucked his little friend down his pants and went out walking. Bare trees cracked, and Arlo Dean, seventeen years old that very night, heard his bones answering.

He didn't want to go home, but there he was, and his father blocked the doorway, talking and talking, trying to make Arlo agree, asking him to promise something.

The little Christmas tree in the corner flashed red and green and blue and yellow—and his mother's face looked flushed and hot, and he just wanted to get inside and smell her. The cold little gun burned his hand, and he waved it in the air before he heard it popping.

*Daddy?*

*Superficial*, the doctor said, *flesh wounds, lucky.*

Arlo was lucky too: six years to serve—assault, not murder.

But Vernon Dean died all the same, ten months after Arlo shot him. So beautiful: *blue sky and high clouds—not cold, but almost.* Lucie Dean found her husband on his back in a pile of yellow leaves. *Peaceful*, she said. *He'd just finished raking.*

Arlo couldn't escape his father in prison: the weary guard slumped in a shaft of light, the big naked man in the shower. That one had grown old and withered, muttering to himself, face gray with stubble. The man stared and spit. *Do I know you?*

One night his father slipped between the bars of his cell. Arlo felt his weight in the room, the shape of him, the pressure of air on skin shifting. This father seemed sad and sorry. He couldn't touch his only son. He didn't have that kind of body.

Arlo tried to wake, to speak, but the dream inside a dream pinned him down until he remembered a long night long ago when he knew this father and loved him perfectly—when the father was kind, and not afraid, and not angry.

The boy must have been four or five, slight for his age, strapped in a car seat. He drifted to the edge of sleep. They could have been driving for days or hours. Time was strange then, a crevasse, narrow at the top, but so deep, so far to the bottom.

Every night was the end of time, the last time he would see his mother. He had two nightlites at home so his clothes wouldn't rise from the floor and float out the window without him. His blue elephant was home too, *safe*, his mother said, but he didn't believe her. Billy Bear was safe—here, on the back seat beside him.

He thought he remembered when the bear was bigger than he was, but that wasn't true now, and it made him sad to see Billy looking so small and tattered, one eye gone, left leg leaking.

He whimpered in his miserable half sleep, and his mother turned and lightly touched him. *Shush, it's okay, almost home now.* Almost, forever and forever, such a tender lie, but it was better, a little—the dark moved over the earth, very kind and quiet—and his parents whispered, and the breath between words made the words holy. His father laughed from the soft place in his belly, and his mother laughed from her throat, rippling—he loved that sound, those two, their music. Laughter was love—for him, and everything.

The sky glowed purple above the tops of trees, and a single hole in the clouds filled with gold light, deep and clear, the last light ever—so kind, the light, to let him see it.

Trees blurred, their bodies becoming air. *Why are you afraid?* Dark in the dark. *You, too—nothing.* He saw the shapes of birds and the shapes of animals, the owl bigger than the fox, the fox faster than the rabbit. He saw the eyes of a deer, reflecting their headlights. She was his alone because he alone saw her, safe at the side of the road. *Tonight, yours, forever.*

He saw the shape of his little hand and the crumpled shape

of Billy Bear who had fallen to the floor on his face, sad and small, half-blind, crippled. Arlo wanted to cry for Billy, but he was too tired, gone from the earth, snatched by sleep, pulled down and under. Then suddenly they were home, and sleep released him.

Daddy unhooked the too-tight seatbelt, lifted him high, held him close against his warm body. Mother said, *I can*, but Daddy said, *I've got him.* He carried his boy up the stairs as if Arlo weighed no more than a stuffed bear or the shadow of a rabbit. *Little One, Belovéd One, you didn't.* Daddy hummed as he climbed, sweet and soft, a song without words, made of breath and vibration, heartbeat and pulse, his own, and his father's.

Daddy must have changed his clothes because Arlo woke into a blue day wearing his blue cloud pajamas. Even now, from this terrible distance of time, the shapes of trees at dusk, the merciful sky, a phrase sung without words can bring back the night, the one night, forever and ever, when love was breath, and breath music.

If he can trust the eyes of a deer, this night is longer and more true than any night that came after. *Now, take me.* If Vernon Dean were here today, alive at the river, he'd whistle through his teeth, and they'd pull Talia out together. Arlo waits for the song to come whole and unbroken.

Ten crows pace the shore. Twelve more from the trees watch them. Beautiful they are—not black at all, but iridescent in this light, shimmering with green and violet. *Please.* They beg him now, voices low and husky. *You might starve in a month, but we could starve tomorrow.* Thin as Talia is, her body could sustain them.

Something touches his shoulder so tenderly he's afraid to turn, to see or not see the shadows of crows, God, his father. *Arlo?* It's Roy McKenna speaking his name, so softly, the big man whispering, so afraid of what it means to find the dog, *oh Talia*, and not find the missing boy, the one he loves, his nephew. *Help me.* He has a rope and a hook, and together Arlo and Roy, these two bound by love, raise the drowned dog from the river.

# 9

## Love Song for the Unsaved Father

You forgive Roy, your crazy uncle. He broke into your house one night looking for his wife and children. He tore the sheets from your bed and the curtain from the shower. How cruel could they be? How scared, how quiet? He dug down deep in your drawers, imagining Tulanie and Iris dangerous as dolls, glass eyes open wide, pretty mouths pink as poppies.

*Don't touch.* He smelled burning meat. *Am I the one?* Scorched flesh. *Did I do this?* Dolls explode and so do children. If he'd found babies stuffed beneath your socks and shirts, would he have breathed into their brilliant mouths, or pulled the pins and tossed them?

Uncle Roy has shrapnel in his back and thighs, a purple scar ripping his chest, a deep puckered hole in his belly. *Inside out*, he says. Thirty-nine years since Vietnam, and even now splinters of shredded metal might rise and pierce through skin, a fiery red rash of sores, a dozen little wounds leaking. Other times, barbed needles fine as glass work their way down to touch the spine, to stab and jolt him.

*Crazy,* Aunt Christine said. *I don't want to want you.* She left Roy three times—once with the kids, twice without them. The fourth time she was really gone, safe at last, married to Malcolm Delacroix, the prison guard she met the year Roy spent in Deer Lodge. White hair, soft belly—Malcolm's hands didn't burn her hips, and the weight of him didn't crush her—easy to be kind to one so grateful, *patient Malcolm,* fifty-two years old the day they met, a wife dead sixteen years, four daughters he'd raised without her. *Good girls,* he said, *two taking their vows, two married.* He opened his wallet. She didn't want to see photographs of motherless children, but here they were—*Brianna, Dawn, Aileen, Ada*—Daddy's girls, silent and amazed, gazing up at her. Christine stood at the window of the Super 8, watching low white clouds move fast beneath gray ones. *I can wait,* Malcolm said. *Almost but not quite forever.*

The tattoo of the Virgin Mary holding Roy McKenna's heart in her heart saved his life or failed to protect him. *Depending on your need for faith, love of God, or bitter loss of Him.* Uncle Roy makes the sign of the cross on his own body: one hand moving head to bare chest, shoulder to naked shoulder—fingers touching scarred flesh so tenderly you think Jesus died today, here, in his own heart, with his mother watching.

The night Roy McKenna lay wounded and writhing, the thick green snake coiling up his left calf twisted from tattoo to life and slipped full of human blood into the jungle. She came back black as the black night, thirty-three feet long, skin glistening. *So hungry.* She held his throat with her hundred teeth and wrapped her body four times tight around him. Did she love his sorrow? She squeezed hard to stop the breath, opened her great black mouth and swallowed. *Everything that hurt stopped hurting.*

He met a rooster and a rat, three wild dogs, seven little piglets squealing. *This little pig.* He felt his toes pulled one by one, heard water over stone, Mother sweetly laughing. All love, all forgiven, everything alive again—Mother not starved to bone, Mother's bowels not twisted with tumors.

Uncle Roy strokes the green tattoo. *I wanted to stay inside you, baby.*

Morning light filtered through broad leaves, soft and terrible—even this, too much, everything so green, the snake dead, her body opened. *Why not me?* Stung, pinched, chewed, bitten—invisible creatures carried him away cell by cell, molecule by molecule. Birds spoke:

*miaow-kieww miaow-kieww*
*popóh popóh popóh*
each note rising.
One sang:
*tirr-ee a-tuu tirr-ee a-tuu*
so joyful—
and another croaked:
*hōk-hak hōk-hak hōk-hak*
to torment him.
*ka – di – di – di – di*
*t'hoop t'hoop t'hoop*
Flash of orange, burst of yellow—birds everywhere, yes, *but*

*they refused to let me see them.*

*kirrhhh    kirrhhh*

At last—

one clear voice,

a glass bell chiming.

He slept and died until a troupe of jabbering monkeys swung down from the trees and carried him to the river. He remembers the noise of them, an argument: some wanted to kill and eat—some to stitch his wounds and save him. He remembers small hands and long tails, rough fingers on his face, one curious macaque pulling his eyelids open.

Who can say what's true? Uncle Roy has barbed wire tattooed around his left wrist and right biceps. *They needed to tie me down*, he says, *and all they had was wire.* A mosquito flew into his ear, and her high, untouchable voice was the last word ever.

He woke on a cot in a tent—bones crushed, brain boiling. *You'll live*, the surgeon said—as if he were God, as if he'd decided. The green-eyed nurse tried to make him drink, but he spit it back: her water piss, her breath poison. *Fine*, she said, *we'll do it this way.* She pinned the arm to pierce the vein. *You need your fluids.* The beautiful nurse opened her black mouth wide and yellow birds flew out of it.

When he woke again, he was soaked in cold sweat, nine days dead, twenty-six pounds lighter. Little monkeys returned—not the jabbering, hungry tribe, not the ones with hands strong enough to crack crabs and pry oysters—not the ones tempted to tear him apart before they dumped him in the river—no, these whispering langurs were thin and quiet, faces glowing gold, dark eyes wide and merciful. *A few more days, a few more pounds, you'll be light enough for us to carry.* He remembers soft fur and blue eyelids. Did he touch? Did they let him? They laughed as birds laugh when no humans are listening.

One delicate female offered her blood. *I'm tired,* she said. *I don't really need it.* He remembered shooting her and her child out of the tree, target practice with Tracy Coake and Vaughn Molina. *Furry little gooks,* Vaughn said. And it's true: their noses were flat, their eyes slanted upward. He remembers especially the pretty female, so bewildered, wounded herself, shaking her dead baby. She didn't feel her insides spilling out. *Look at that,* Tracy said, *friggin' miracle.* They watched her die for half an hour.

Two nights later, out on spook patrol, hearing ghosts, smelling monkey, Tracy Coake tripped a wire—triggered a daisy chain booby trap strung with American grenades and coconut shells full of glass and nails. Roy knew he should hit the ground, but he reeled and tried to run, to go back, *before,* to a cool place down the path where this thing hadn't happened. He rose up out of the mud, a man illuminated. The sniper waiting in the trees missed his heart, but found his belly. *Inside out,* Vaughn said. *The little bitch got all three of us.* Vaughn had a hole in his face where his eye should have been.

The third time Roy woke, the tent was not a tent, but a high canopy of broad leaves so dense and green only the faintest light touched him.

    *ti – tu – tu    ti – tu – tu*

    *pseet  pseet  pseet*

*What does it mean to die?* Everywhere on earth birds find you. He was shivering now and so thin he felt his bones fizz and sparkle. *Fourth of July*, Vaughn whispered as they watched their bodies exploding. A bird too bright to see said:

> *kh'ree ki'yew   kh'ree ki'yew*
> and with a clear, sweet voice
> he answered.

Pain is its own light. Roy McKenna lay shining.

Orange snakes flared their ribs wide, flattened their sleek, speckled selves, and flew limb to green limb, swallowing lizards. Five red-eyed frogs caught flies on tongues twice as long as their brilliant green translucent bodies. Ferns everywhere grew taller than a man, wide enough to hide a bear, a child, a tribe of monkeys. One scarlet bird showed herself at last:

> *aaaiou – ooo   aaaiou – ooo*
> and the river ran slow
> with red clay,
> slow enough
> to count the bodies.

The doctor checking the wound in his belly said, *This one's your ticket home, Private.*

Twenty-eight years later, Uncle Roy still needed every gram of marijuana found in his possession—93 grams to be exact—smoking numbed the pain—just enough, just a little. The judge could have sent him down for twenty years, but gave him five—three years, nine months suspended. *I'm considering*, he said, *your unusual circumstances.* He meant shrapnel and flying snakes—jibber jabber in the skull, monkey blood in the vein. *Is that a child with melted flesh? Is that a hand? Is that a face?* He meant mothers who can't die, birdsongs that don't cease.

While Uncle Roy mended fences on the prison ranch,

Aunt Christine was at the Super 8, letting Malcolm Delacroix console her. Two kestrels whirled high, and the prisoner knew what he knew: the crying birds told him.

You were six when Uncle Roy broke into your house, eight the day he went to prison—nine the night Iris was lost, twelve the day Christine was married. She expected the children to choose her, but Tulanie refused to go, and Iris said, *My brother needs me.* Did she see the future: a boy flying from his bike, birds trembling as shadows? Did she imagine Tulanie falling from the sky, limbs splayed, back broken? If you ask her what she meant, Iris says, *Our mother left us—that's what I remember.*

You remember Uncle Roy on his knees, hammer in his hand, mouth full of nails—a man bending to his work, calm at last, strangely grateful—a father humbled by hurt, building a ramp for his fifteen-year-old son's wheelchair. There were birds, yes, but he couldn't bear to listen. He let the hammer speak: one word at a time, one word over and over.

Sweet Mary Mother of God slit the man's violet scar to slip her own bright heart inside him. She took his in return, though it was small and dark, the color of rust, five times pierced and still bleeding. *Enough,* she said. *Let me love you.* She's not afraid of grief. *You think I don't know?* Tulanie's pain has lifted Roy's rage out of him.

Today, or any day, Uncle Roy might find the wheelchair at the bottom of the stairs. His crippled son has crawled up to the attic room where he used to sleep, where you and he climbed out on the steep roof to leap or fly, to fall unbroken, boys stunned to bliss, angels in the snowbank. Tulanie's opened the window wide—a threat, a promise: *I could again— any day—but today, for you, I didn't.*

Tulanie's injury is incomplete, T12/L1, the spinal cord torn, but not severed—*here*, low on the spine, just where the back begins to curve, where Tulanie can't bear to be touched, the place where he feels slowly stabbed, the border between what is and what isn't. *Half man, half cripple*—he loves the word—he makes you say it. He shows you his catheters and gloves, *proof*, he says, not an hour he forgets it.

Tulanie lifts his left foot two inches, sweat beading his face, hands gripping the wheels. *Steady?* he says. *Higher than yesterday?* You nod. You don't want to lie. You don't want to hurt him.

Hours later, Tulanie pounds his own legs to make them stop throbbing. *Why is there pain where he's numb to sensation?* You walk home through the park, near the pond, by the willows. White roses wave, the wind wild all around you. Such a strange, cool day, the sky darker and darker—hail pounding the grass flat, hail tearing the roses—you fall down bruised in the wet grass, so grateful to feel it.

Any night, Tulanie might be down the ramp and out alone into the world. He drinks himself dumb, till the legs don't work at all—not an inch, not a quiver—till there's nothing to want: no hope, no torment. The hot stab becomes a sweet burn—*a friend*—a warm pulse radiating down his groin and through his buttocks, a light he can see, rays separate from himself, moving down the legs, shining out of him.

One morning last August, you and Uncle Roy found Tulanie's chair thirty feet from the bike path, tipped on its side at the edge of the river. *Gone*, you thought, *this time forever.*

You loved Tulanie before you were born, each in his mother's womb, kicking and twisting, already trying to touch, sensing the other—Tulanie and Kai—*love, always love, closer than brothers*—you heard your mothers laugh, birdsong under water.

He lay half a mile down the shore, naked as the day—half scorched, half frozen—body burning on the rocks, legs dangling in the river—Tulanie still too drunk to care—convinced his legs were only weak from cold. *Screw you*, he said. *I'll walk home later.*

He couldn't remember how he'd lost his clothes, if he'd given his shirt to a homeless boy, or if Neville and Trina had stripped him. *Pissed myself*, he said. *They did me a favor.* The kids love him in their way. *They're not afraid of some freak in a wheelchair.* They share whatever they score or steal: fifth of tequila, flask of brandy—dope laced with monkey dust that makes them whoop and jabber. If they take his clothes, it's only fair: they have beautiful legs, but Tulanie has his father.

They're not unkind—just unpredictable. Another night they might wheel him through the dark streets, leave him in his own front yard, cover him with a blanket. Rikki might kiss him for free, might whisper a love song lullaby: *Hush little baby, don't say a word, Mama's gonna buy you a mockingbird. Hush little baby, don't you cry, Papa's gonna find you by and by.*

Another night, Trina might strip fast and leap in the river laughing. Neville might ease Tulanie Rey into a shallow pool where limbs torn from trees block the flow, *safe, here*, where the current swirls. This holy night Trina swims close enough to touch, and Tulanie's back does touch her cool belly as he dives under and swims away, arms stronger than they've ever been, a boy quick as a fish, sleek and silver, Tulanie unborn, restored by water.

How many times will Roy look for his son, bring him home, wash him? How many mornings will he not scold while he checks for cuts Tulanie doesn't know he has, bruises he can't feel?

*Seven times. Seven times seven. As long as I can. As long as I'm able. Till you choose.*

*What?*

*To love yourself as I love you.*


The night Uncle Roy broke into your house, you and your mother found him curled on the couch, harmless now, exhausted by his rampage. The green snake coiling from ankle to knee twitched, but the barbed wire around his arms kept him from thrashing.

Your mother covered him with a sheet, and you tried not to look too hard, but he felt your heat in the dark and woke more afraid than you were. *I'll sleep here,* he said, *watch the door, fix the lock in the morning.*

He stared at his big hands—as if they were the ones to blame, as if they had made him do this. His torn shirt gaped open wide enough for you to see one blue unblinking eye of the Virgin Mary. *I understand,* he said, *if you need to press charges.*

*And tell the police what?* your mother said. *That my sister makes you crazy?*

You remember your uncle washing his hands at the kitchen sink, water so hot your mother had to stop him. In the morning he sat on the edge of your bed, rolling your socks, folding each one of your little boy t-shirts—everything so small in his hands, dangerous as dolls' clothes.

He lay the soft shirts back in the drawers as if cloth were skin and he could hurt you. Uncle Roy moved like a man trapped in mud, a soldier swallowed. He spoke from the belly of the snake: *I didn't want—I didn't mean to scare you.*

He put one hand on your narrow chest, spreading long fingers wide, burning his imprint into you. Yes, you were the child lost, the body recovered, the son found alive and whole, the baby wailing in the light—the belovéd not burned, not blown to pieces.

Now, again, here, you feel it: the weight of his hand, his hand on you underwater. You know if Roy comes in time, he will raise you up, breathe into your open mouth, speak your name and save you.

# 10

# In This Light

*P**lease come.*

Tulanie's trapped: ramp slick with ice, sidewalks crusted deep in snow. He's pulled himself free of the wheelchair and crawled two flights to the attic room.

*Now.*

He doesn't know who he wants: *God, Kai, Iris, Mother.*

He wants to hear Talia bounding up the stairs—the dog alive, his father mistaken. How slowly does the heart beat under water? If Talia could survive, Kai might follow. Joseph said, *There's no reason why some bodies float and some bodies fail.* Joseph the Jumper, that's what Tulanie called him. He'd been in the spinal care unit at Harborview five months when Tulanie got there. Joseph Trujillo flew from the West Seattle Bridge, snapped three times and lived—*blessed,* he said, *no reason.*

Tulanie wants the pigeon in the attic to die, or rise up and fly out of here. He's flung the window open wide, but she won't go—she won't leave him. Three days she's stood, trembling in the shadows, refusing to speak, refusing to take the bread crumbs he's tossed her. She's leaking blood and water—clear pink fluid dribbling from wounds he can't see, flesh he can't heal.

Outside, brothers and sisters mourn:

coo – cura – coo

coo – cura – coo

She might be the holy ghost of one he wounded years ago, *before*, when he was fast on his feet, a boy with slingshot and stones, bow and arrows, *so quick*—his limp legs twitch, remembering. He speared lizards and snakes. He shot robins and squirrels. He never considered pain until his body shared their sorrow.

*Please.*

He wants Neville and Trina and Rikki to blow into his house and steal him. *Now.* Take whiskey and milk, venison and chocolate. You don't need to snatch bones from junkyard dogs or risk your lives eating garbage.

coo  ca – doo – ca – doo

Don't sell your skin tonight. The door's unlocked. Lie down in every bed and choose your favorite mattress.

*oo – whooo  whoo*

Take my mother's clothes—blue nightgown crumpled in a drawer, wool coat hanging in the closet. *Everything, please*: towels, boots, pillows, toothpaste—take my featherbed and all our blankets.

He wants the children warm tonight so he can stop shivering.

*Is this love?*

Jesus spit in the blind man's eyes, and the man saw the suffering of the world. *So, here, be well, be humbled.*

Neville says, *Everybody's lost, sooner or later.* If he ever had a home, Neville Kane can't remember. He does remember a blue tub and red blanket, a gutted school bus down a ravine, broken glass, no tires—Mother too wasted to work, Mother too sick to keep him—Jessie Kane old at twenty-six, smooth brown skin gone dry and yellow. Neville remembers his uncle's house, a windowless room in a basement, water weeping down the walls, a green sleeping bag, a damp mattress.

*So, here, be good.* Mother kissed him on the mouth. *I'll come back when I'm better.*

Is this why the bird stays alive, to make Tulanie witness? *Please.* He could ease the pigeon's grief—now, end it—shorten her days, complete her hours.

*woof woof whoo*

The ones outside urge or forbid him. He'd need a rock or a shovel, strength in his hands and heart, unflinching will, absolute focus. He'd have to crawl to her to do it, drag his pitiful legs behind him—Tulanie Rey, on his belly—humble, yes, bowing down to her.

*Not your will. Nothing when you choose it.*

It's easy enough for a clever boy to pump pellets from his BB gun—to wound, to maim, to slaughter—but it's not so simple for a cripple to catch and stab, hammer and strangle. You have to love the one you kill—you need to know she wants it.

Who is he to decide? Maybe the pigeon loves her life, *this life*, even now, so diminished. Maybe she waits day by day for the hour when the light reaches her at last, one ray of light, warm and transient.

To kill the bird now, before she chooses, he'd have to frighten her, cause the sudden grief of fear and struggle, the bright stab of pain as she twists and flutters.

*oo' koo – koo – koo*
*whoo – oo  whoo – oo*

No wonder the others cry, sensing what he imagines.

Joseph the Survivor said, *You don't know if you want to die until somebody offers to help you.* Joseph Trujillo stood on the West Seattle Bridge leaning out and leaning back again, stalling traffic, in and out—*now, do it*—a dozen times in a dozen minutes, trying to decide: *Is this a good day to jump, or should I wait for another?* How could he know? Even tonight there might be some secret blessing: clouds full of coral light, bright water reflecting them. How can a man think with horns blasting?

*Jump.* He found the place he wanted—high enough, a way to the water—he wouldn't hit the tangle of roads beneath the bridge, wouldn't fall to Harbor Island. *Do it.* If he waited too long, a fireman would save him. *Now.* The ones stalled in their cars wanted Joseph Trujillo up and over the edge, out of their sight, *gone*, one less heap of trash soiling the world.

*Please.* He didn't intend to cause them trouble.

That morning, in his tent under the freeway, down deep in the jungle of hemlock and pine, swordfern and maple, Joseph washed his whole body clean with rubbing alcohol. *So I wouldn't smell too bad, so I wouldn't dirty the water.*

Good today not to dig in dumpsters, to stay hungry, to die

light and full of God, almost clean, needing no man's mercy.

*Bléssed are you who hunger now.*

*Jump, you idiot.*

*No human hand will ever hurt me.*

> *raow raow*
>
> gulls cried:
>
> *Come to us, now, do it.*

He looked back to see the mountain rising out of cloud, disconnected from earth, only the peak of Rainier visible. *How can you bear to leave this world?* Was this the mountain's voice, or had the sturgeons come from the sea to catch him? *Look at you, the light on your hands, just now, so beautiful.*

After the rubbing alcohol, Joseph dusted himself with baby powder. The smell of it kept him on the bridge. *Mother.* Before he had a word for her, he loved the first salty sting, the warm stream from her nipple.

*You can die tomorrow.*

He heard sirens wail, but the ramp was clogged—the police couldn't get to him. *Joseph.* He could still go home, *please,* one more night, *can I sleep here?*

So kind Mother was the last time, finding his favorite flannel shirt, pulling white towels from the cupboard. He caught a filthy beggar in the mirror—torn trousers creased with mud, black hair hopelessly snarled.

*Jump.*

The shower burned, hard and hot, tiny pellets. *Please.* He was afraid of the body in the mirror, skin scorched raw, bones chattering. Those clean, quivering hands couldn't hold a razor. *Help me.* Father oiled his face and shaved him smooth. *Why speak now?* Mother took him to the porch and snipped his wild hair down to soft curls. *Home: everyone alive in the merciful light of evening.* Joseph watched fine strands of himself lifted by wind, stolen by sparrows. *May you never die.* Nathan Trujillo smoked a cigar, and Joseph took the smoke of his father into him.

*Love.* They loved him even now: the birds, the wind, the light, his parents—but the child lost and found and full of smoke slipped free six hours later. *The sheets hurt, too blue and busy.* He stuffed a plastic bag with Spam and tuna, a pint of cream, six oranges.

He stole twenty dollars from his mother's purse. *Please.* He sensed her lying in the dark, holding her breath, breathing only when he did. Mother with her eyes wide: *Anything you want, take it.* She heard the plastic bag crimp and crackle, felt his hand slide into her purse, his fingers slip into her wallet. *I'll weep when I die—a cold, black river.*

Joseph pressed down the keys of the piano so tenderly hammers struck wire but made no sound, left no chord trembling. A cool breeze moved through the house—Joseph gone again—*no matter how much we love you.*

*Do it.* Were the people on the bridge trying to help him? A woman in a white lab coat floated through the clog of traffic, cloak full of light, long and loose, open in the wind, flapping. *It's only water.* Yes, but the water chopped by waves looked dark and hard, and the gulls cried *No*, and the snow on the mountain glowed pink, and the sturgeons promised to carry him far, and the wolf-eels promised to eat him.

In and out. *Now.* Three firemen sprinted between cars, running to push or grab him. *Please.* Two boys leaped from a truck. *Is that a baseball bat? Is that a crowbar?*

*coo – ca – doo   ca – doo – ca – doo*
*One boy wanted to kill, one hoped to save me.*
*ooo – whoo*
Pigeons cried from under the bridge
and Joseph the Flier flung himself free
to be with them.

He heard the song he didn't play, soft as light, light on wa-ter. *This can't be death.* He saw the backs of gulls. *So beautiful to soar above them.*

*Yes, the water's dark, but the eyes of flounder gaze up at you.*

Even if the stunned firemen and curious boys were leaning out to see, even if the woman in white spread her wings and dove to catch him, Joseph Trujillo could not spin fast enough to see his savior. So close now, the water—so cold the air above it—too late not to die, and so he tried to be good, *very good*, forever and ever. Hard, yes, hard as stone, gray as granite, the cold water rose up, and the stone of water broke him.

Did he hear the neck snap? *Three times, but the water never killed me.* Joseph Trujillo lay face down in the Duwamish Riv-er, waiting for rockfish to rise or cormorants to swoop down and take him.

*oo' koo – koo – koo*

Three hundred pigeons mourned, but he couldn't raise his head even a centimeter to hear them.

*Bless you, this body, broken by wave, fractured by water.* Lan-tern fish glowed in the dark. *Don't be afraid.* They'd come from sound to bay to river. *We'll light your path to the bottom.*

So close to life, *all life,* here at the end of it. Mother and Fa-ther swam from shore to touch their only son, to witness. *No crying now—you can't weep in water.* They couldn't turn Joseph to the air without severing his spinal cord. He would die this day, *soon*, lungs pierced by splintered ribs, spleen ruptured. *No lullabies—please, I can't hear you.*

He felt clouds watching their backs. *See how small we are?*

Fish, sea, sky, mountain.

His parents were the cold waves so sweetly numbing him. *Now, nothing more—rock me unto death, rock me on the water.*

Something black and terrible rose up. *Not your will.* Three beings came, eyes huge and blind, tanks pumping oxygen. *Don't save me.* They didn't feel the surge of Joseph's thought roaring down the river. *Please.* The lantern fish fled. *We can't help you.* One man swam on each side, one dove under him. This creature had arms strong as a vice—*to clamp my head and flip me over*—one iron arm down the spine, one straight down the sternum. The others slipped a stiff board under him—*stabilized my neck and strapped me tight*—head and chest, knees and pelvis.

*Blesséd are you who thirst for air, who gape empty.*

Joseph couldn't speak or breathe.

*You who died have been delivered.*

Two men on the boat raised him up. They had a mask and bag to start his breath, oxygen to flood him. *Don't be afraid.* The divers lifted their own masks and peered at him with human faces. Light slanting through clouds touched the men's hands as they touched him.

*Love—no matter what you've done, no matter how dirty.*

He tasted blood in his mouth, felt front teeth shattered.

The five prayed to the one broken: *Just stay with us.* And he did stay. *Because they wanted it. They risked their lives to save mine. Who was I to take it from them?*

*Blesséd are the broken.*

*Blesséd are the merciful.*

Joseph died three times in the hospital. *And each time Jesus came and laid his hands on my chest and jolted me.* It makes as much sense as any other explanation. Joseph the Jumper, three times dead, three times fractured, arrived in the spinal care unit at Harborview Hospital in early March, and Tulanie Rey arrived from Montana in August. *There's no reason why some bodies float and some bodies fail.* Tulanie was a flier too, nothing spectacular—not a bridge or a cliff—*only a bicycle.*

Joseph should have been paralyzed from the neck down, should have died when he hit, or drowned in the river.

*Jump, you idiot.*

*Blesséd are you when men hate you.*

Thirty-eight years old, seventeen years homeless—Joseph Trujillo survived the walk across the bridge, the hundred-and-fifty-foot fall to the water.

Isn't this enough of a miracle?

*Jesus held my neck in his hands one night while the rest of you were sleeping.*

Joseph whispered in the dark: *If you wish, you can heal me.* And Jesus said, *I do wish it, but I'm old and tired.* It was true: the man's hair was thin and white, his long beard full of feathers. He pulled a chair to the side of Joseph's bed. *I'll just wait with you awhile.*

In October, Joseph Trujillo walked on his own two legs out of the hospital—no metal frame to hold him straight, no crutches, no walker—his left leg felt weak, his right hand tingled. *I'm not asking you to believe—I'm asking you to witness.*

Joseph was free to live under the Interstate again in a tangle of blackberry bramble, nightshade, and holly—free to build a house with sticks and tarps, cardboard and plastic.

*Blesséd are you who live off the trash of the lucky.*

Joseph Trujillo was free to dig a pit and line it with rocks and build a fire—free to eat his dinner out there in the wild woods with ten thousand birds singing his name and ten thousand cars roaring above him.

Joseph Trujillo was free to die another day—Tulanie read about it in the paper—not Joseph, but one like him, another scrap of a man doused in kerosene, despised and mocked, set on fire—murdered by boys like Tulanie Rey, fast on their feet, quick and cruel, children who on another day might have gone to the woods to spear snakes and shoot squirrels.

Why does anything die? How can anyone murder?

*Are you better than a bird, more clean, more holy?*

The pigeon who won't die waits for the light to reveal her luminous body. Tulanie feels it now, her pain, the place he's broken, his own spine stabbed, a fizz and burn down his legs, sharp ribs piercing. He's the one with the knife, and the one in the gravel twisting.

*Please come.*

*You're not going to die today.*

*Please.*

*No, I'm going to kill you over and over.*

*Coo – cura – coo*

*Now you know.*

*What?*

*How it is for all the others.*

*Please.*

And something does come—not God, not his cousin Kai missing now eight hours under the ice in the icy river—not his sister Iris, face burned by cold, fingers half frozen—not his mother who left her voice at the edge of sleep and her smell in every closet—not Trina who let him kiss her naked legs down by the river one holy night last summer. No, none of them come to this room in this hour. Talia doesn't bound up the stairs to shake her wet fur, to spray, to lick, to love him. The pigeon doesn't rise and fly, doesn't offer proof: *Yes, even now, all things in me are possible.*

*Please.*

Only the light comes, and the bird who has stood in shadow all day stands in the miraculous light, washed clean, head shimmering bronze and pink, throat flickering green and lavender.

Everything rises up. Everything dies after.

The bird offers herself to him, feathers alive with light, whole body trembling.

Last summer, Rikki and Trina and Neville stole Tulanie's clothes and left him drunk by the river. All night owl spoke to stone, water to willow. Before she ran away, Trina let him kiss the smooth hollow of pale skin between the bones of her pelvis. Never, never will he feel himself moving fast inside her— but when he touches Trina's legs, his own legs shiver.

*Is this love?*

Every blade of grass leaves its imprint.

Nothing is separate now, nothing outside the mystery— *rock, cloud, tree, river*—Tulanie's body made whole by the bodies of others.

*Please.*

He didn't want the day to come, didn't want God to find him naked.

*You can't say my name softly enough.*

Kai helped Tulanie's father lift the broken boy back into the wheelchair.

*Your most tender touch destroys me.*

Who is he to choose life or death, to imagine Kai on one shore or the other?

*Until I see you with my own eyes, until I touch your numb or radiant body.*

> *coo   ca – doo – ca – doo*

*Blesséd are you who wait, who hope when hope is impossible.*

The light holds the bird, and the boy beholds her wonder.

He remembers Dorrie Esteban in the tree house, gold dust swirling in the light, Dorrie's skin sparked with gold fire—one child protected by the light, *Dorrie Esteban,* the first and only girl he and Kai loved together. Impossible to imagine that child not alive, a winter day eight months later.

She pulled her shorts down far enough to reveal the bloom of violet scars high on her hipbones.

*Beautiful,* he never said, *like flowers.*

*What would you give to kneel in that light and touch her?*

*Heart, hand, eye, liver.*

*What would you give to raise your cousin to the light and save him?*

Dorrie Esteban gave her brother Elia the dark core of herself, bone dreaming bone, sweet marrow.

*Please.*

*If your blood could save this bird, would you open a vein and let her drink you?*

Two years after Elia died, Dorrie Esteban flew into the windshield.

*What would you give now to touch her wounds, to hear Dorrie whisper a word, to know that secret?*

He remembers pounding on her mother's door, circling the little house, throwing rocks at the window. He wanted Oleta to come roaring out, *alive*, fierce with what she'd lost—not one, but both her children.

*Destroyed and destroyed.*

She sat by her son's bed. She drove the car the day Dorrie shattered the windshield.

*Please come.*

Tulanie hammered hard with both fists. He needed to see Oleta's face, bruises and stitches—as if he sensed the time to come, his own future: legs limp, Kai missing. He needed to understand who to be, how to live, what to love, *after*.

But she refused to show herself to him. Oleta Esteban did not open the door—*no, never*—did not part the red curtain—*not once*—did not press her holy, unhealed face to the glass—did not step into the wild, unbroken light to curse, to love, to bless him.

# II

## Love Song for the Mother of No Children

You followed Oleta Esteban every time you saw her. At the grocery store she was buying frozen peas, milk and bread, chicken broth, two bananas. Is this what women ate after they lost their children? Oleta looked as if she scavenged crumbs left for birds, seeds scattered. Brittle, she was, an old child, thin bones beneath yellow skin suddenly, terribly visible.

You remembered her in a red dress and white sandals, Oleta before Dorrie and Elia died, arms bare, toenails painted. She dropped her sandals in the dark grass to dance with her children barefoot.

Dorrie Esteban gave her marrow to Elia but failed to save him. Nine years old, she was, the same as you were. *Too close,* the doctors said, a match too perfect. Dorrie's cells didn't recognize any part of her little brother as dangerous. Everything in Elia was good, even his cancer. *Florid,* Doctor Botero said, meaning the leukemia bloomed again, wild inside him.

You turned eleven, flush with love, falling in love with Dorrie Esteban. In a tree house she'd found deep in the woods, Dorrie showed you and Tulanie the scars on her hips where needles plunged to draw marrow out of her. Roof of sticks, floor half rotten—the tree house rocked in the wind, a broken cradle. Rays of light opened every crack. *Nobody saves anyone forever.* Light touched Dorrie's hips and hands, and passed through her.

At the river you skipped stones and felt blood thin as water rippling through you. Elia did live, five months longer than expected. Twilight streaked the sky rose and violet. Frogs sang from trees and swallows dove, catching insects. *Everything loves life: frog, bird, boy, mosquito.* You heard the fluttery *whoosh* of your own heart, valves opening and closing. *Is this all we are: wings, stone, water, twilight?* Dorrie's marrow flowed through her brother's veins to find its way inside his bones and become part of him.

When she said she was going to die, it didn't surprise or scare you. *Sometimes I see myself walking toward myself, and I just feel very beautiful.* All day you wanted to touch, but failed to touch Dorrie Esteban.

*Very beautiful.* She did die—in the car, with her mother—a cold, bright day eight months later. Nineteen-year-old Kelly Flynn, blinded by the glaze of ice, late for work and helplessly hungover, hit the gas to run the light at Meridian. Oleta slammed her brakes hard with both feet, but the green Dodge clipped Kelly's white truck and spun into the light pole. *Why does any child die one day and not another?* Dorrie's seatbelt snapped, and the girl you loved flew into the windshield.

Three minutes earlier or five seconds later—they might have never met Kelly Flynn if Dorrie hadn't taken time to kiss and wake her father.

Now it hurt Oleta Esteban to walk on bones shattered. Why would God need all her children—not just Elia and Dorrie, but Amalita too, the little one never born, cells flushed away, blood whirling down the school toilet. Oleta Riero, still a girl living in her parents' house, just fourteen the day Amalita went back to God, the dirt, the crows, the river. For seven weeks Oleta carried the child of her father's cousin. *Uncle Paolo.* Only her sister knew, and that night in the bed they shared, Graciela laid her hands on Oleta's heart and belly.

*You've mended well,* Doctor Savoy said, *better than we expected.* He meant her feet and face, her ribs, her pelvis. At the grocery store, sixteen months after Dorrie died, Oleta used the rolling cart to steady herself as she moved down the aisle. You were thirteen, drowned with love, in love now with both of them.

There were things she touched but didn't buy: oranges, mangoes, powdered chocolate—a peach pie with a lattice crust, peanut butter swirled with scarlet jelly. What did Mario eat? She can't remember. Does her ragged husband shop for himself, or is he starved hollow as Oleta? You imagine their bodies in bed, bone piercing bone, no comfort.

Perhaps Mario eats at the houses he tends, the faithful caretaker devouring whatever people leave behind when they fly to their other homes in Montreal or Capistrano, Marseille or Kailua-Kona. He keeps nine houses now, respectable work for a man raised as a migrant. Mario remembers a night so dark and full of stars he thought God had swallowed him—

Mario Esteban, seven years old, alone with his mother and father, silent and blessed, these three crossing a field together, the smell of mint impossibly sweet and strong in the night air, tender leaves rubbing his dark feet, the sweet smell becoming him. His sister Serafina had stayed in the tent with the baby so that Mario could go to the river, so that he might be loved and known, this one night, cherished as an only child. The wind was still warm, but they were cool and clean, and the stars fell into the black curve of the hills, and the stars above swirled. They were safe and dark as the night. Nothing was not God. Nothing could hurt them.

All day Mario Esteban might be hot and dirty, coughing from dust on the fruit they picked, choking on pesticides. He might drink from a shallow ditch winding through a field. All day he might refuse to eat, sick and hot and full of poison. But tonight, he was washed clean and hungry, and he knew when they returned to camp they'd find a dozen fires blazing, pretty girls dancing with old men, little boys with grandmothers leaping. They'd move from fire to fire, eating tomatillos with chipotles, eggs baked under hot rocks, beans fried with chorizo. Jalapeños, mulattos, pasilles, habaneros—his father's mouth would burn, and Mario would run to bring him wine and water. They'd eat masa cake with caramel cream, the goat's gift, milk thick with honey. All night Mario's body would throb with the guitars, skull jangling like a tambourine, drums talking to his bones.

And this too would be good—but now, in the field, even the crickets stopped chirping, and the silence was God, and the stars were inside him. Mario Esteban had never been so good, so loved, so clean, so perfect. He remembers his father walking ahead, Aurelio Esteban becoming the shadow of himself, not quite visible—inside the night, not separate from it, Papá reaching the fence first and starting to climb over. Mario's legs felt suddenly weak, chilled by the cold river. He was small in the great dark night, hungry and tired—but he knew when they reached the fence, his mother would lift him high and pass him to his father, and his father would feel how tired he was, and kiss his hair, and carry him.

Mario saw the flood of light and flash of gunfire, understood the cry of the gun before he heard the farmer's warning. Aurelio Esteban clutched his leg, shot in the back of the knee, halfway over the fence, snagged in wire—Papá shot a second time in the hand, and a third time in the shoulder.

Mario's mother knocked him to the ground, and he didn't breathe because he couldn't breathe, and he didn't move because she pinned him. Every leaf of mint stood alone in the light, every thing on earth terrible and separate. He thought he'd die of his father's wounds, that the smell of mint would drown him.

Aurelio Esteban never walked straight again, never danced with Serafina—never picked cherries with his right hand, never reached over a fence to carry his son Mario, never rocked in both arms the baby Tobalito—never lifted, Mario's mother said, anything heavier than a bottle.

Today, or any day, a day in late June when you followed Oleta Esteban in the grocery store, Mario might be on the far side of a secret lake, high in the hills, with a view of the mountains.

The house he tends has a private road: *Turn Back Now. No Trespassing.* Mario has a key to the wrought iron gate, a whole ring of jangling keys—nine gates, nine houses. *Look at you,* his father says. Mario never knows if the dead come to praise or mock him.

Each bedroom here is bigger than Mario's house. Thirteen children could sleep in one bed, a hundred hungry migrants hide in one closet. There are 327 bottles of wine in the cellar, and to the man who owns this house, each one is precious. Mario sees wine splash in the dirt, hears one bottle break, his mother's curse, his father's weeping—Mario Esteban feels his own skin torn, and tastes the blood of children spilling out of him.

He won't go down the stairs today, won't check the temperature of the cellar. He won't open the closet doors, though he's supposed to check for leaks and bats, spiders and squirrels. He's afraid to meet a hundred dark faces in the dark, muttering to a hundred gods, praying in a hundred languages. He's afraid he'll recognize one face, Mario Esteban still seven years old, dizzy with the smell of mint, terrified and silent.

He stays in the light beneath vaulted ceilings. One side of this house is an eighteen-foot wall of glass, held tight between timbers thick as trees, raw wood meant to fool the hand and eye, left bare to look like cedars growing. It's Mario's job to keep the glass clean and gather birds that fly into it.

*Turn Back Now.* Rosy finch, meadowlark, bluebird—these three failed to heed the signs. The wild robin did not comprehend where sky was not the sky, where clouds did not belong to him.

Mario's made a soft pouch of a tattered t-shirt, and he uses this to carry the birds back into the forest. He leaves their small bodies cradled at the roots of trees, safe in beds of dirt and needles. Mario keeps his faith: the bobcat will come tonight and make the birds part of him.

No one is safe in the house or the forest. *Trespassers Will Be Shot.* The long leather sofa is softer than Mario's skin: smooth, dark hide scraped clean from the bison. *Private Property.* He lies down, suddenly so tired, one hand touching the pillow he can't use, fur of the fox: *Violators Shall Be Opened.* He hates himself for stroking the deep fur, loving the red fox, forgiving the killer. He wants to slice the skin free, fold it back into the shape of an animal.

A whitetail doe stands just beyond the glass wall, watching this befuddled man without pity or judgment. Does she see inside, or is she in rapture, mesmerized by the elegant grace of her own reflection?

Mario needs to be home, now, cradled in a narrow bed in his tiny house—every curtain drawn tight, every window locked. He wants Oleta's skin touching his skin. She won't speak till night comes. The door to their children's room is always shut. They don't see the bunk beds Mario built, the flowered sheet Dorrie hung to hide herself, the blue ladder Elia climbed to sleep high on top. Their little boy loved to touch his glittering glow-in-the-dark stars, the heaven of twinkling light Oleta so joyfully and without fear pasted to her children's ceiling and walls.

But Mario can't go home. There's work to do: beds to strip, tiles to polish, fireplaces to clean, a Jacuzzi to drain, the refrigerator to empty. And he's hungry now—too hungry to notice wind riffling the deep lake, water flashing turquoise and silver.

You imagine Mario Esteban, hard-boned and stringy. He sits in the yellow glare of the open refrigerator eating soft white cheese and smoked salmon. Neither is a delicacy to him—the cheese sticks in his throat, the salmon's too sweet and salty. He's full after three bites—full and hungry. He gnaws on a cold lamb chop, cut thick but very small, so rare it's almost blue at the center.

The departed have left Mario two miniature cakes made from the white flesh of the flayed rattlesnake. Did the snake trespass here? Did his rattle betray him? Who caught, who cut, who cooked this creature? If he eats the snake, will Mario be condemned to slide along the earth, forever breathing dust, forever dirty?

Should he dump the cakes, or bury them? If he leaves them for the crows, will the birds forgive and bless him?

The missing have left ten truffles for dessert, dense chocolates flecked with gold leaf, real gold—he could eat these and die, belly ringed in light, bowels gilded.

The disappeared drank wine from glasses so fine they have no weight, only shape and color, faint echoes of topaz or emerald—amethyst, tourmaline, fire opal—each one perfectly impossible, molten glass hand blown by a blindman in Palermo. Their jeweled light spills, sparking veins of quartz hidden in the granite countertop.

The five glasses have been left out to dry, for Mario to see, to touch, to want, to carry silently and without haste or harm to the cupboard. He's afraid to breathe now, afraid a fragile glass might slip from his trembling hand, might fall and shatter on slate, might glitter brilliant as sapphires. Mario hears bright bells of breaking glass as if the thought of his crime has made it happen. Once the breaking begins, how will he stop it? He sees the cellar flooded with wine, birds flying into the house, glass clouds and blue sky on the floor in splinters.

He washes his hands, but they stay dark, palms wide, fingers clumsy. Are they clean? Is it possible?

He's shaking now and decides to wait, to move the glasses when the sun is low and their dazzling light stops tempting. Mario hears muttering in the closets, prayers of the dead, the dead trying to protect him. Mother, father, nine aunts, six uncles—three grinning grandparents blissfully blind to their children's future—thirty-two never known, half-loved, dark-eyed cousins—Mario feels them very close—the missing, the dead, the left behind, the not forgotten, the too old to walk with goats across the desert—he hears the unborn children of his children, Dorrie and Elia—the ones forever lost and still so hungry—Mario eats for them, cracking quail eggs into his open mouth, chasing them with pomegranate juice so brilliant he feels his bones dissolve to light, ribs and fingers glowing. Mario Esteban eats glistening caviar by the heaping black shiny spoonful. Nothing sustains, nothing fattens. His children starve. They murmur in the walls; they tap beneath the floorboards. But eating like this for the dead, stuffing himself sick, keeps them from wailing.

At the grocery store where you followed Oleta Esteban, a tiny child strapped in a cart whimpered. Her plump pretty mother had walked away to find the perfect avocado. Momma fondled and squeezed—too hard, too soft, too black, too pale. The girl's little body clenched and shivered.

She didn't want to cry, but the cries rose up and out of her, strange fluttery sounds—too high to make the woman turn, too soft to bring Mommy back to her. Oleta stepped toward the cart, thin back quivering. You saw her shoulder blades, sharp as wings poking. You were afraid she'd snatch the child and run, that her fractured feet might break again, ribs snap, pelvis shatter. Still she'd flee, lifted by the child's cries, pushed beyond pain by the small heart hammering. Oleta swayed side to side, already sensing the girl's body pressed against her own—pale skin soft as something inside the body, and the smell of her, sweet as sugared almonds—you felt her too, this holy one, this living child.

You meant to step between and spare Oleta Esteban more sorrow. She didn't reach or touch, only trembled. You couldn't see Oleta's face, but the little girl grew miraculously quiet, green eyes wet and wide, tiny hands opening and closing, as if she sensed something in the air, something too fine and light to see, something only the starved mother of no children could offer.

You remember Oleta Esteban's hair, a dark wing curved against her small body. You wanted to slip your hands under her hair, but you turned away, afraid even your wild thought might hurt her. Now, cold as you are, numb to the marrow, you want to lie down in a small dark place and let the black wing of Oleta's hair cover you.

PART THREE

## 12

## Lost Children

Oleta Esteban walks a narrow path above the river. She's not here to save the boy. Where ice breaks, water flashes. She's come for the ones not taken, the motherless children who've searched all day and still hope: *We might be the first to touch you.* They see a boy shivering in the woods or floating naked down the river—lost like them, ashamed of what he's done—open-eyed, waiting.

Who is she to doubt? They don't believe in God; they know him: river, ice, cloud, mountain—God, the breath they share with birds—cold, the wind whirling through them.

Tejano bounds through the woods across the river—sable and gold, a dark flurry of dog, leaping in and out of light, blond legs shimmering. Full of joy, he is, even now, at this hour—homeless too, one of the strays who sleeps with the children. Cave, ditch, box, basement: home to him is wherever they are. *What thick fur you have!* Tejano keeps them warm all night, lying in love in his dog dreams between them.

Last week he found Rikki in the snow, dumped at the side of the road, half-buried—his favorite girl numbed to bliss, heart barely whispering. Tejano nipped her frozen hands, then jumped on her chest to jolt her. *Born again*, Rikki says, *that crazy dog in my face, digging me out, howling.* So good to go down in the cold, so terrible to wake and warm after. *Every muscle cramped hard, skin split and bleeding.* The dog licked her ears and eyes. *Damn you, Tejano.*

Oleta knows the animal's smell in Mario's truck: blood and earth, muddy paw prints. Tejano drags the chewed leg of a deer into the yard, drops a stunned rabbit on the doorstep. She finds his happy splatter of prints on the bedroom window. *What delicate feet you have, Tejano!* Peeping dog, he's stood on his hind legs to watch the humans in the little house: the tiny woman who cradled the rabbit till it died, the stooped man who buried the deer's leg in the woods.

Tejano dances across the pane, hoping to dazzle the woman he loves. Night after night, Oleta slips outside to leave gifts in the unlocked truck: peanut butter and bread—baby carrots, milk, bananas—liver for him to chew, a tough knot of rawhide bone. He smells skin and hair, her sweet musty trace lingering on fleece blankets, bandages, socks, gloves. If Oleta Esteban is ever lost, Tejano will find her body or her clothes, lick her back to life, or howl till Mario comes to save them.

Rikki ties a long wool scarf around his head and neck, holds his furry face in her hands, kisses his wet nose. *What big ears you have, Tejano!*

*Yes, the better to hear your heart murmur under snow.*

Tejano doesn't sense Oleta now, across the river—he's

caught something else in the wind, something closer, a scent of deer so strong he whirls. Invisible, they were, ghost gray, standing still in blue shadow. Now they crash through tamarack and pine. *Perfect joy!* The whole earth trembles. Tejano doesn't want to catch—five deer with flashing hooves could turn and trample. *What soft flesh, what bright blood, what wet fur you have, Tejano!* Their warm breath fogs the air; five hearts flutter through him.

Oh, this whole happy day down by the river! He's flushed twelve deer, harassed three weasels. *Yes!* One day free, all his children out in the woods, wild with him in the cold world walking—his hungry people not dragging him downtown, not making him sit in a box to help with their begging. *Please, for Tejano.*

Oleta's seen them outside the grocery store, has watched busy mothers brush past, faces turned, mouths frozen. *No, nothing.* She's given them apple juice and bags of oranges, fifteen dollars she's saved or ten she's found in a house where she scrubs floors and scours toilets. She doesn't steal. But if a crumpled bill falls from a pocket as she's sorting laundry, if dusty quarters roll into her path as she vacuums under a bed or down a dark hallway, she accepts the gifts in the spirit they're offered.

She'd never keep anything for herself—not even the dangerously soft pale pink cashmere sweater Natalie Dupree so generously pressed into her hands one morning last December. *Too small for me,* the woman said, *but you're just right, so tiny.* Oleta gave the sweater to a child five inches taller but almost as narrow through the ribs as she is—a thin-but-not-fragile girl with green eyes and blue fingernails—Trina, hair streaked orange and red as if she's just caught fire. Yes, that one loves the spark and roar: bonfire on a beach, doll in a field—white sheets on a clothesline billowing into blaze, two trashcans torched in the school bathroom. *So much waste in the world!* Not sorry—no, never. *That's why,* Trina says, *Grandma couldn't keep me.* She carries cotton balls soaked with Vaseline, a waterproof box, a hundred matches. She'll save her friends a hundred times, gather sticks, feed the fire.

Oleta sees her now across the water. She's with Neville and No, and a blonde girl in a turquoise coat—the little blonde isn't homeless, not yet, but she's unpredictable as the dog—and like him, half wild. The girl follows Tejano into the woods, as if the boy she loves might be here, hiding behind trees, whispering her name to scare her. *Iris.* Nothing, no one—only pines singing in wind, and the happy dog giving up the chase to run circles around her.

Tejano yips and dances, bounces high and snaps the air, waiting for the girl to toss snowballs. Why won't she understand? He wants to leap and catch and crush them. Such a small thing to give—but no, she can't be taught or tempted. Iris climbs down to the river's edge, chasing the reflection of clouds, the shape of a boy scattered by water.

No yips with the dog, spins and dances too, gives Tejano what he wants, a flurry of snowballs that sends the dog four feet off the ground, body twisting. He could die this way: too happy—heart too big to hold, ribs bursting.

Neville Kane slides down the bank to stand beside the girl, to wait for Iris to see what he sees: stones in the riverbed, reflections of trees plunging deep, clouds rippling below them—waits for her to hear, *yes*, birds everywhere around them: kinglet, nuthatch, chickadee, creeper. *How do you survive one day, one night of winter?*

Softly, they answer:

> *t'see t'seep*
> *t'sick – a – dee – dee – dee*

The tiny nuthatch toots like a tin horn, climbing down the tree headfirst, walking on the undersides of branches—unafraid of Neville Kane, of gravity, of Iris. The little brown creepers can make themselves invisible, wings and tails spread, mottled bodies motionless—but today they spiral up the trees:

> *t'see – see – titi – t'see*
> *Yes, we know, we're watching.*

Dangerous to love one child more than another. Neville Kane—he'll break Oleta's heart, disappear one day, disguise himself as dirt and rain, a bird fluttering to earth, one brown leaf falling. *You won't find me when I die.*

He's cinched his pants tight with a rope, but they flap loose around him. *Stolen, yes, from a scarecrow.* Neville: six-foot-two and still a child, seventeen years old—maybe a hundred and thirty-five pounds if you fill his pockets with rocks and weigh him with his boots on. His torn jeans ride three inches above his skinny ankles. He's made himself with broken pieces: stitched and glued, wired and bolted—if Oleta rolled Neville's socks down, would she see the brown legs of a boy, or discover bleached bone of a deer, stripped limb of a willow?

*Neville!* He's pierced holes through his lip and nose, ears and eyebrow. He loves the quick pain: jab and jolt—blade, needle. Beautiful, this boy, tangled hair dark as deer moss. *Pulled it from the trees, and now the deer follow me everywhere.*

Is it true? She's seen doves fly from the cuffs of his jacket. Neville's hands flutter when he speaks, rise and open to reveal pale palms, long fingers—impossibly long and loose, every part of him. One day he held his arm out to show Oleta, *yes,* Neville Kane's arms, nine inches longer than hers are—thin muscles strung tight, tendons popping—Neville's blood violet in the vein, the pulse of him fast and visible. Oleta could hardly breathe with the boy this close to her.

She can't confess to God or Mario.

Neville sees her watching him across the water, looks down at his scuffed boots, grins to thank her. They're good boots, almost new, too wide, but long enough to fit him. Oleta found this gift in Cyrus Tuvelli's basement. No use to the old man whose feet had swelled up red and purple. He was going to lose them or die—that's what the doctor said.

She could have asked for the boots, but she didn't want to hurt the old man or explain to Anya, the daughter who still believed her father might walk by spring, might kneel with her and dig in the garden. Anya sat on his bed, cleaning raw sores, humming softly.

Easier just to set the boots on the back stoop, snatch them up hours later. It was wrong for the old man to cling to things he couldn't use—a kind of theft from the child who walks miles every day, who needs the boots now—not next month, not next summer—not when the old man loses his feet and the daughter stops pretending.

Dangerous to love. Better to sing or be still, crouch or cry, hide in the bathroom. Oleta remembers kissing her own father's mouth, one last time, *Hasta mañana, Papá.*

Oleta's grateful when she's on her knees—scrubbing grit, breathing ammonia—glad for the work and the will, amazed to have the strength to do it. Yes, her bones hurt, but isn't this proof: the body loves its shattered self—the broken body wants to heal.

She knows if Anya Tuvelli caught her slipping even one tattered handkerchief into her pocket, she'd be done, gone—nobody in this town would hire her. Soon enough Mario would lose his jobs too: one by one, keys reclaimed, the faithful caretaker and his brittle wife no longer trusted. They'd lose the truck and plow, the little house, the bunk beds Mario built, the once too red but now torn and faded soft pink rag of curtain—still scarlet, *yes*, too bright to touch, *here*, at the edges.

A stranger would take the earless goat, his wife slaughter the six chickens. Oleta imagines the rooster grieving as roosters grieve, smelling blood in the dirt, scratching hard to keep them close, to hear them squawk, his poor, betrayed, murdered family.

They'd be migrants again, gathering morels or huckleberries, avocados and pears—pecans, serranos—asparagus, mint, artichokes, tulips. They'd sleep in a box, a shack of sticks and twine, a tent sewn from a tarp, a house built of tin and cardboard—Yakima, Fresno, Eureka, Lampasas—they'd lie dreaming under swirling stars, naked in an orchard, Mario's skin smooth and damp, Oleta's beautiful bones unbroken. If God heard them making love, if Oleta dared to laugh in disbelief, would He turn his head in shame and give her one more child?

*All I have is yours.* Trina, Neville, No, Iris—chickadees flittering close, kinglets flashing—creepers falling like brown leaves, Tejano's heart racing. *All I am.* Five deer in the woods, invisible again, watching. She's scared now, suddenly cold. Where's Rikki? She's seen the girl—not once but many times—cruising the west side, waiting for strangers—an old man alone or two not-so-old dressed like brothers: black shirts and faded jeans, boots sewn from lizards—both with the same tilt to the hips, the same battered-by-wind way of walking. Crippled, quick, young, withered—who can say; who remembers? *What long legs, what bright skin, what big hands you have, Daddy.*

So small she is when they finally meet, when she stands beside them: Rikki Kruse, a pretty little girl in tight jeans and fake fur zebra jacket—a slender animal, *yes,* twelve years old, almost a virgin. *That's why,* Rikki says. *Not like a woman at all, nothing to scare them.* She climbs into a white truck, a silver Cadillac, a red Camaro. She never knows where they'll go, how long they'll need her. They dump her thirty minutes or three hours later, face bruised, mouth smeared dark with purple lipstick. *It's not so bad,* she says. *Sometimes they get me high. Sometimes they buy me breakfast.*

*All I am.* Oleta promised herself not to love other women's children, but here they were one day in the park, Rikki and Neville dragging a drunken man into the cool grass, to hide him in the shade, safe from little thieves, safe from wild boys on skateboards. *You never know,* Rikki said—*maybe Jesus, maybe Daddy.* The pigeons fluttered down to see, and Rikki touched the man's face with her fingers.

*All I have*: a child knocked from a swing, too stunned to cry, lying on his back, breathless—*yours*: a dirty, barefoot girl climbing fast up a willow to snatch one beautiful blue egg from the nest of a robin. *All I am*: the robin who swoops and cries, the child who flees, the blue egg dropped in the grass, miraculously unbroken. *Yours*: the boy who came to her house after Dorrie died—the relentless, cruel one who pounded on the door, who pressed his ear to the pane, who waited and waited. *No.* Oleta curled on the floor, eyes closed, ears covered. *Please.* Now she would open the door—now she could love him.

Rikki, Trina, Neville, Iris—No, the boy who can't drink milk—No, the boy who won't take chocolate. Oranges burn his mouth; seared flesh scares him. *Grass*, Trina says, *sticks and bark, stones and lichen—that's what No eats*. Oleta watches him waver in the wind across the water—Peter Fleury, a child so fine and fair a whirl of snow could take him.

*Yours, to love, today, by the river.*

She tried to die, tried to follow Dorrie and Amalita and Elia. She walked into the woods one cold October night, nineteen months after Dorrie died, 594 days after she took her last child's last breath inside her.

*hoo – too – too*

*hoo – too – too*

The little owl watched. The coyote followed. The aspen felt her warm blood and leaned toward her. Then the rain came, and her blood ran cold in the rain, and the trees thought she was one of them walking through the woods unrooted. The rain talked leaf to yellow leaf, needle to needle, and she loved the rain, and she was never going to stop listening. But the rain did stop, and the clouds parted, and the moon followed her through the trees, face half turned, half in blue shadow.

She knew Mario would come, that even now he moved toward her. The owl flew so close she felt his cry inside her.

*hoo – too – too – tōōk*

Her children didn't need her now—to them, now was the same as forever. She thought of Mario running through the woods all night—Mario living tree to tree, minute to minute—trapped in the terrible torment of time, tripping on roots and rocks, tearing his jeans, tearing his bare hands open. *Querido!*

One bird began to sing, and the sky began to open, blue between the limbs of trees, wisps of coral clouds swirling. *Are you the body or the song—blood and bone, or air trembling?* Dorrie's hair brushed her face and arm; Dorrie one more time kissed her. Elia stood naked in the light, the water of him still in the air—gold and green, rose and violet—each cell a prism, but so much pale sky between, and then the unbelievable ripple of song, the bird's voice exploding through him.

Amalita was the ache inside, lungs and heart, pelvis shattered. *Never gone, never not with you.* Oleta swayed side to side, rocking her. *The night is never long, never dark enough to heal.* She knew that what her children wanted most today was for her to go home and love their father. She did go, *yes, she does love* him. She looks for Mario here, a small, dark man across the river—Mario with his strange faith, his hope at the end of every day, his need to find a living child.

Neville, No, Trina, Iris—one by one they've vanished: No up a ridge with the dog; Neville deep in the woods, deer watching; Trina and Iris down the shore, running now as if the lost boy cries and only they can hear him. *Please.*

She wants Mario to come—from the other side, the other direction—to kneel in the snow, to spread his arms wide, to catch the children if they want to be caught, to hold them if they can bear it.

*Yes.* She wants to tell Mario how it is to love the lost, how much it hurt the first time. So afraid, she was, smelling a little boy's smell, raw and sweet: wet leaves in the woods, torn blossoms in a field. She remembers wiping his fingerprints from the mirror, dusting the glossy black rocking horse in his bedroom—cleaning his mother's house, promising not to love him. *What big teeth you have!* The animal reared and rocked with the slightest touch, wild eyes watching her. The hurt in her hands and ribs called her back into her bones, and the bright stab of pain saved her. *No,* she wouldn't love—but there he was, the boy, the shape of him in the bed, the crumpled sheets holding his imprint. She wanted to lie down in that bed. She wanted to die there. *No.* The real boy came, alive, face smeared with mud, bare feet filthy—five years old but small for his age and not bound by human language. He stood in the doorway watching her work. *Yes, you, little master.* She waited for him to go, or bark out some ridiculous order. No, he stood—so quiet, dirty hands close to his chest, one over the other. He had something precious and small inside, something he wanted to show her. She touched the thick tail of the black horse and set it madly rocking. *No.* She turned her back to the boy, furiously dusting—but he stayed—she felt him—unloved, unwavering. Why had he chosen her, and not his mother? Light through glass blinded her. She sank down on the unmade bed, and God let this child come to her. His belly touched her legs. In one ragged breath, she smelled all of him—dense and damp: black mud, grass, lilacs. He rested his arms on her thighs. *No, you'll kill me.* The boy opened his little hands like a shell, just wide enough for her to see the green frog, eyes popped wide, skin glistening. *So beautiful!* Alive, this strange being, smaller than a walnut—here, in the boy's hand—here, watching her. *Is this how the world begins?* She laughed, *yes*, as if for the first time: that sound, that cry, one hard breath erupting out of her.

The boy clamped his hands tight and ran, but she felt his soft body all day, arms and belly pressing into her—she smelled blood and milk, dirt and sugar. That night she found grass in her hair, crushed lilacs in her pockets.

*Mario!* If he comes, she'll tell him now, this secret—a hundred children to love, a hundred thousand. *Look at them!* A girl in a green parka, a boy in desert camouflage—*yours*: this ripple of bright clouds, this flock of birds rising. *Querido!* She wants to comfort him as Dorrie comforts her. *Isn't the fox watching from the woods? Isn't the bear still sleeping?* Dorrie speaks in riddles, but her voice is clear, water over stone shimmering.

Elia says, *I'm going to close my eyes now. You close your eyes too, and we can just sleep here awhile.* Were these the last words, or only the ones she remembers? She lay her head on the sheet next to him, and with his small hand he stroked her. *Mamá.* Twice he touched—and then nothing more, no more words, so tired.

They lay together like this, all day, the last day in the hospital. Cold outside, but hot in the room—she remembers blinds drawn, sun blazing. Gulls flew close to the glass, wings wide, only the silhouettes of gulls visible—not terrible to see, not comforting—themselves and not themselves, the shapes of birds, shadows.

Elia opened his eyes. And wasn't this love, proof of love, the gulls they saw together? All words, all strands of words lost, but the shapes of birds—never.

And then it was night, and Elia was the one who decided *when*, who chose *no more*, who took one long breath and not another, whose blood pumped away from the heart and did not return to it.

*Isn't the body of a flower still a flower? Isn't the smell of earth sweet, sweeter than all roses?*

Another hour gone, nine hours lost this boy in the river. Now birds rise and part—sing in flight—dive, regather. Into her mind blue and wide as the winter sky, the boy's thoughts come as birds, the shapes of birds, the prayers of bodies—as songs that change the shape of air, as music passing through her.

*What is there to love if not everything?*

Mario appears—just as she imagined, walking on the other side, walking slowly toward her. He's found the child, pulled one lost girl back into the world: Rikki Kruse, alive another day—not sleeping in the snow, not beaten, not buried—close enough to touch—Rikki in her zebra coat, shivering.

What can Mario do? He sees Oleta, but there's no bridge to cross, no way to reach her—only the long shadows of trees, falling shore to shore, rippling on the surface. *Useless, this love.* The girl ignores him. He unbuttons his wool coat, touches her shoulder—waits for her to decide, to turn or not turn, *yes,* to grab, to take it.

*All I have.* Oleta walks with them—down the other shore, but in the same direction.

## 13

## Deer Song for Juliana and Roxie

You were never going to die.

Late last fall you climbed trees with your father, cutting dead limbs, healing the forest. The whole world was yours: curve of earth—

sky, mountain.

Love came as sparrows: a field of song at the edge of the forest.

No words all day—only the buzz in your skull, handsaws humming through pine, whistle and slur—no thought but this:

cradle of tree, wind rocking.

Sixty feet from the ground, but you were strapped and belted, not afraid to fall, not afraid for your father. The pulse of the tree sang through bone and muscle.

Clouds closed over the sun, scattering light to a rim of blue, blue of the whole sky pulled to one blaze above the mountains. Snow dusted the ground below, but sparked hard on high peaks, so cold it burned, so bright you felt yourself falling into the blue: air too thin to gasp, eyes unribboned.

Pines swayed in wind; your harness held you. One crow swooped low enough for you to hear its wings, feathers riffling air, blur of black—but no cry to jolt your heart, no half-human voice to save you.

Only a moment, this little death: face struck by light, pulse in your neck

fluttering—

and then the earth gray and calm, the sky safe again—no need to fall, no desire—layers of cloud tinted green and lavender, hiding the blue edge—quiet clouds sinking low, holding you safe in the tree, sheltering snow and mountain.

You sucked air deep into your lungs—breath so hard it hurt, so cold the crow's voice burst out of you.

Your father spoke your name, called to you from a pine up the slope, touched his mouth and waved from high above, and you raised your hand to him as if nothing had changed, as if you hadn't died and returned—*here*, while your father watched you.

Later, in your father's house, love was Juliana standing on her hands, Roxie turning cartwheels—love, their long hair sweeping the floor: back handsprings, dizzy somersaults. They wanted to ride you up and down the stairs, but Angie said, *Not tonight, your brother's tired.*

*Brother.* The word pierced and opened you. Love: not something you choose to give, but something your sisters with quick hands and whispery voices lift lightly out of you.

*Little thieves!* They snatch the bandanna from your head, slip the buck knife from your pocket. Nine-year-old Juliana sleeps in a tattered rag, your stolen t-shirt. Roxie tromps through the house in your big boots—barely seven, she is, pretending to be you, carrying your handsaw over her shoulder.

What have you done to deserve their devotion? You hide in the woods behind the house, and your trembling sisters come running after you. You spin them in the yard, holding one arm and one leg, turning silent Roxie and then whooping Juliana into flying squirrels. Roxie stands on your shoulders, and you two together are tall as a tree, miraculously unrooted, walking as a tree might walk when only owls are watching. You let them bury you in the snow, or tie you in the closet. You rise from the dead and chase your squealing sisters in circles.

At the water park, the little girls whip down the winding tube of slide twenty-nine times, till they're too numb to speak, too tired, till their thin bodies shiver—though the day is fierce, sizzling in August. You bundle them in big towels, rub their feet hard with your hands, blow your warm breath on their fingers.

In return, they give you their whole selves: their trust, their love—kisses on your neck, wild ripples of laughter.

Kisses, yes, they steal these too, take the taste of your skin on their tongues everywhere. Beautiful, you are, perfect one, only brother. You belong to them. This love, this life, these children whose blood you share, these small hands on your face, this November night of perfect peace—you warm at last after a day high in the trees, crows swooping above and sparrows singing beneath you—now in this fire's leaping light, smell of pine, bark crackling—you come into the world alive, called by the only name that matters: *Brother*.

Yes, this is why: everything you love tonight only because your father left you.

*Please.* Your sisters grabbed your belt and wrapped themselves around you. Juliana clung to your right thigh; little Roxie gripped your ankles. So tired, *yes*, face flushed, hands weirdly hot and swollen. Your bones throbbed, saw still whistling through wood, the core of you still buzzing.

But you gave yourself to them, let them ride you like a pony—took first one and then the other three times around the living room and down the long hall and up the stairs and back again before you fell to your knees and said, *I can't, no more, I surrender.*

What is love if not your sisters pushing you all the way down so they can lie quiet at last, one on each side, breathing as you breathe, *here*, by the fire?

In your father's house, you ate venison steak and mashed potatoes—green beans, sweet carrots—bread torn from the loaf, apples baked with raisins and cinnamon: earth and air, root and animal.

You remembered the deer hanging in the shed, belly slit, blood dripping—now her flesh was here, taken inside you and your people. Griffin's deer—how could you not love, how could you not want her—this one, the doe he tracked five miles through snow until she stopped and turned as if listening. They stood so close he saw her ears twitch, felt her huge lungs swell with breath, and his own breath rise out of him.

Snow began to fall as clouds watched them.

Griffin might follow an elk three days, climb four thousand feet—up one ridge and down another, sleep in a cave of snow—melt snow and drink it. The elk might circle back to follow the man, bring him within a mile of home, slow their pace, appear and disappear, turn as if to say, *We're almost ready.* Griffin could hold the animal in his sights and still decide, *Not this one.*

He can't explain why he returns with two grouse or one rabbit.

The doe left her tracks fifty feet from his cabin. She used her hooves and nose to dig down to sweet roots and lichen. She tore at the bark of fir, and ate the needles of juniper. An easy day—he thought he'd kill her within a thousand feet and was almost ashamed to follow.

Branches snapped and snow whispered.

He entered a warm space between trees, the pulse of her body still lingering. He lost her tracks twice—once where the earth lay bare and hard, and once where the doe bolted in thirty-foot bounds across a meadow. Easy to lose him now—if she chose, if she wished to do so. She could leap an eight-foot fence, fly above a gully.

Foolish to come so far for one like her: men shoot deer in their back yards; girls with guns kill from their bedroom windows. The deer have grown dangerously tame, grazing in gardens, stealing apples from orchards.

He followed because she led, because the crows flew limb to white limb, seeing her from above, urging him along, waiting for the man to open and offer her.

He'd climbed two miles from the cabin before he found

fresh tracks, ones not blown by wind, not half full with snow whirling. She was close, he knew it—maybe standing just ahead, stopped in her tracks, sensing the shape of him in air, warm ghost of a man pushed forward.

Griffin—he's afraid in the grocery store when he sees skinned meat pale in plastic, spare ribs of one being, pink loin of another—breast of a bird cleaved, two dozen legs in one package. Where are their heads and necks? Who pierced their hearts and livers?

Almost dusk, five miles from home, and Griffin knew he'd be spending the night here, gathering sticks, starting a fire— scooping a cradle in snow, sleeping on soft boughs, wrapped in a silver blanket. Yes, all this way—she wanted to show him: *You might be the one to die; I might choose not to save you.* She was gone in the dim light, ghost gray in gray woods, the shapes of trees already blurring. Even the crows had abandoned him. *But might return if I return and use my hooves to open you.*

Why did she wait when she could have slipped free, one last sprint, ahead of all parting? *You are the one.* He couldn't believe. Even when he saw her standing still, he thought, *No, dreaming.* Snow swirled down, flakes spinning and touching, five becoming one, two bouncing hard and breaking. Was she as stunned by snow as he was, seeing how sometimes it rises up, catches a gust of wind and twirls?

In that moment, all things still possible:
flight or death, the rifle raised
or the man
charged and trampled.
No words, no thought in words, only snow falling faster

now, snow falling on pine and spruce, fir and hemlock—snow drifting down on a man's face, snow touching softly the face of the animal. And later: blood frozen in the snow, crows squabbling, crows heavy with the heart of her, full at last in dark trees roosting.

Was he afraid to kill?

*Yes, always.*

The voice of the gun filled the forest. Even now if you stood in this place, you might hear strange music: every ring of every tree somewhere deep inside trembling. Such a song in you: rush of blood in the vein, aria of cells dividing.

Griffin slit the belly of the doe, touched lung and rib, bowel and bladder—dragged her entrails across the snow, let the birds take these parts of her.

*Never gone, never not with you: crow, tree, snow—always.*

All night, Griffin stayed close to her open body, drifting in and out of sleep, listening for coyotes.

Light released him. She was cold now, no longer herself, no longer waiting. He made a sled of sticks and twine and dragged the body down the mountain. *You are the one.* Even dead she might have killed him. Dawn to dusk: the man had no choice now that he'd taken her.

Days later, Griffin and your father spent four hours in the shed, slipping their hands under skin, sawing through bone, cutting sinew from muscle. You remember how dark she was inside, the flesh firm without fat or gristle.

Three months since you took her into your own mouth, into your own body—now she's flesh and bone, every cell transfigured. You're everything she was: clear water from a mountain stream, wild onions dug from a meadow—bark, seed, root, needle—mushroom, apple, corn, clover. She's Angie and Tim, Juliana and Roxie. This small doe fed your mother and Theo—Griffin, Roy, Tulanie, Iris. She fed the crows. She flies over you. This one bounds through snow, hidden in you, disguised as Talia.

What is there to love if not the one who gave her life, whose body has become yours, whose spirit now sustains you?

# 14

## Retreating Light

Theo's escaped.

All day he's listened to Lela scrub and vacuum, upstairs and down—in every room: his daughter singing. She's stripped the sheets and done the laundry—dragged Kai's crumpled clothes from under his bed, found the dirty heap hidden in his closet: twisted underwear and limp t-shirts—her seventeen-year-old son's filthy jacket—a bandanna dried stiff, used last night to stop a nosebleed—the smell of earth ripe in his clothes—torn jeans crusted with mud, dappled gray with Talia's footprints.

All day that sound: water churning.

The washing machine in the basement jumps and spins; the hardwood floor hums beneath them.

She wants everything perfect when Kai comes home: faded shirts folded in the drawer, socks paired and rolled together. She asked Theo to help—but *no*, he won't—*no*, he didn't. She makes the bed alone, smoothes clean blue sheets, tucks the corners—turns the fleece blanket down, makes a nest of three pillows.

*He'll be cold*, she says—*and so tired.*

She brings the down comforter from her own room, because Kai's green quilt is thin and tattered, stuffed with fiber gone flat, not full and warm with feathers. *I should have bought him one for Christmas. I will*, she said, *tomorrow.*

Is she mad?

Her hope destroys him.

*Please.* Theo tried to speak, but she pressed two fingers to his mouth: *Don't—we don't know yet.*

She has chicken breaded and ready to bake, cream of potato soup simmering—cornbread in the oven now, honey on the table.

*He may just want to sleep tonight, but tomorrow he'll be hungry.*

She won't leave the house.

*No, I need to be here.*

*Lela!* Always his cheerful girl, *little bird*, his youngest—born eight weeks too soon: no fat beneath the skin—all head and brittle bone, blood and bruise, no sound from her, *God's to love*, no breath, no whimper.

*I thought you'd never cry.*

*I thought I'd lost you.*

Even now, drifting to the edge of sleep, Theo sometimes feels her there, sweet weight against his chest and shoulder, heart to fluttering heart—Lela home at last, *alive*, his child. *Such a voice you'd found inside!* Beautiful to hear, lungs full of air. *A howl bigger than your body.*

What is love if not the night, the soft, wet snow of April, your child saved by some grace you don't deserve, some divine miracle? *Hush now.* Theo walked in the garden with Lela beneath his coat. *So Naomi could rest, so you wouldn't wake your brother and sister.*

What is love if not scilla blooming wild in May, here, against the rock wall, flush of blue surviving late frost, clusters of tiny bells so cold they're almost ringing?

White bark of weeping birch, yellow limbs of weeping willow—buds of the cherry glowed rose; hawthorn broke to bright blossom. *What more proof do you want?* Fir, spruce, pine, juniper—everything alive again, new and green, a blaze of green, morning light through fine new needles. Theo walked tree to tree—to touch, to smell—tears welling. Early June and even the tamarack turned though he'd seen the yellow needles fall, a rain of gold last October.

He wants to hold her now, wants Lela small and without words, the smell of her close: sweet scent of sweet peas spilling from their silky blossoms. *Lela!* Bluebirds sang before dawn. All day vireos warbled, hiding themselves high—leaf and light, wind and shadow, *love*, the black locust full of song, the birds all day invisible. *You gave me this*: swallows swooping low, the air chittering at twilight.

Not like Griffin and Christine who loved Naomi first and then each other, who had no need of him, no desire. He remembers that hungry boy with his tiny stomach. Naomi up six times a night—half killed by love, so thin and dizzy. Griffin drained his mother dry, but couldn't hold her milk inside, always sick and squalling after. *Don't go.* Theo never said—but the words pounded in his brain, the thought, yes: *Griffin owns you.*

Christine wanted to feed herself as soon as she could hold a bottle. She was walking at one, packing a lunch and running away from home at seven—riding a bike at five, the back of a motorcycle at eleven. Griffin found her in the brambles or the basement, ten miles from home or perched on the roof, watching. Griffin caught his nine-year-old sister leaning out from the bridge, testing how far she could go, how long wind will hold a child's body. They walked home through the woods at dusk, both fierce with what they'd seen, never sorry.

What is love if not the one so frail she can't refuse you? Lela Mikaela Hayes, born the first hour of March, tended by nurses, washed by strangers. *I saw you take your first milk from an eyedropper.* She lived in a plastic box. *I wanted to touch—they wouldn't let me.* The hummingbird comes to sip from foxglove and Sweet William, drinks from the hollyhock, opens the snapdragon. *Lela!* Thirty-nine days apart. *Skin so fine you looked translucent.*

He did not risk joy—joy besieged him: Lela home after all this time. His to love, his to comfort. *I was the one in the night—always.* He never says, *Your mother died the day you were born.* Never confesses: *Six pints of blood it took to bring her back into the world.* Three days before Naomi spoke, and each day he thought: *This must be the last one.* He won't let himself remember the bargains he made, trying to choose. *Wife or daughter.* The smallest poppies bloom gold and orange, opening themselves to light, waving their shattered hearts in a bed of violet iris.

God gives you both, *just this once*, to crush and spare you.

Lela seemed huge today, standing at the door. Who was this woman? *I forbid you.* She could have said, *Please, Daddy, don't go.* Could have pounded his chest with her fists or fallen limp against him. *Why didn't you jump in the river and die? Why didn't you die or save him?*

But no, even with the light almost gone, she won't ask these questions.

*You'll freeze,* she said. Yes, he will, so cold already—father and daughter trembling now—cold air rushing in, back door cracked open.

A touch could have brought him to his knees.

*Don't—we don't know yet.*

Hours since those words, and now the cold stands dense as a body between them. Kai's body lost, Kai gone nine hours.

*Go then.* She didn't say, *Go out there.* She stepped away from the door, let the retreating light, the wind be his companions.

So they are. And they will hold and rock, or clutch and kill him. Gold light burns through trees. The wind knows him blind, the cold feels him naked.

Theo stands at the edge of the river, tries to remember where but cannot find his own tracks trampled beneath the footsteps of hundreds. He remembers the blue beam of his flashlight illuminating the tracks of deer early this morning— a skiff of snow on ice, ice near the shore thick enough to hold the animals. *What have you found?* He remembers Talia rolling in scent. Fox, vole, feral cat—stray dog, two coyotes. The whole world here—just for her, just created. Talia punching through snow, begging Kai to follow—remembers losing them, and finding Kai's tracks, later—seeing how they stopped at the edge of the ice—the place, *yes*, not believing—water rushing beneath ice, a whirling welter of sound, Kai and Talia gone, ice broken—remembers an old man, his own body, feeling his slow, stupid self stumbling in his own footprints backward.

If he could find their marks in snow, he might undo this: bring back the fox and vole, save the drowned dog, raise the child up and breathe into him.

*No.* Too many footprints now, too many strangers. He sees a tribe of shivering children—bare hands, bare heads—dressed in coats two sizes too big, stolen from the bin outside the Salvation Army, frayed by moths, torn at the shoulders. Two skinny girls in pants too tight, two boys in wet sneakers.

He knows them, some of them—has seen them diving in dumpsters after dusk or crawling out of the Salvation Army bin at midnight. Throwaways thieving filthy clothes. Children eating garbage. Any of these twelve might be the same strays he's tried to ignore outside the grocery store, the ones who use their dog to turn the hard of heart: *Please, for Tejano.*

*No.* He never flipped them a dime, never once tossed a crumpled dollar. *What can one man do?* Seven hundred homeless children. *Is it true?* He's heard that many haunt this valley. He's failed to love even one, failed to see, failed to imagine. *What are you to me?* Have they come to shame him? Have these twelve hungry, half-frozen children searched all day for his child? *Why do you love one and not another? Why Lela and not Christine, why Kai and not Tulanie? Are we not yours?* He feels the children watching. A narrow man paces the pounded path on the ridge, carrying a tiny girl in a pink coat on his shoulders.

*One of the belovéd, one of the lucky.* Her little coat, her hood with white fur, her round face flushed with cold shatters him.

*Why have you come?* Hundreds here, even now, silent pilgrims, loving the lost boy, loving one another—believers moving up and down the shore on both sides, still hoping—footsteps like prayers laid one inside the other—hundreds whispering to God as if he might come down as wind or light and change this—as if he might appear disguised: the air they breathe, the space between them. Theo sees some circling back, knows others search miles beyond him. Kai no longer his alone. *Our son, our brother.* Wind through trees, deer watching. *Why not now?* Snow shaken from limbs, snow falling.

Is this the pity of God?

The wind blows through, the cold burns him.

The child has been found and lost a dozen times today, seen tangled in roots or high in treetops—floating downstream, encased in ice—Kai Dionne, the limb of an elm broken. He crouched at the river's edge, staring at his own reflection. That child saw blue of the blue sky, naked limbs of weeping willow. He ran into the woods with seven deer. *If you find me now, I'll be half wild.* He walked fast at noon, heading north on Main Street. That ragged boy pulled his hat down over his ears, tucked his chin, and kept moving.

*I don't want to come home tonight. I don't need you.*

He appeared sleek and wet and quick as an otter. Showed his smooth dark head, stared at the pitiful humans. He'll never understand their grief—the strange, hopeful ones—the lost, the deluded. Do they think they can catch him now? He's in love with water. He gazed at their eyes with his eyes; he saw them reflected. He loved them as God loves: without desire for any one in particular. He dove down again and under—disappeared beneath ice again and again and forever.

No one knows this river.

Some say it is fast, some say slow and winding.

Where do you stand when you speak?

What hour have you come, what season?

Here it riffles shallow over stones—here it's shining silver. Beneath the bridge this river runs deep and green—under the road it roars between boulders. Wider than a city street, narrow as a rutted alley—here a tree has fallen, limbs jammed, water pooled and frozen. Here the river splits and a shallow thread of ice winds into the woods before a pile of stone stops it. This river reflects pink clouds in pale sky at dawn or swallows the moon whole, black mouth wide, cold throat open.

Snow piles softly on ice, and now it is safe to cross. Here you might have run across the ice a hundred times this morning. A boy could have jumped hard on ice, full weight of him hammering. A dog might have skidded across frozen water, bounded up the far shore, never catching the clever squirrel.

In March, open water reflects brittle yellow grass and the rose-colored limbs of river willow. In January, ice holds the green of dark pine, casts it back not as tree, only as shape and color. Today, the third day of February in the hour before twilight, a boy might be snared in ice or submerged in clear water—might be hiding in plain sight—here, barely five hundred yards from the place it happened. Theo knows: so easy to hide if you need to do it. He sees four cars embedded in the riverbank, rolled down from the slope above, rusted, half-buried, so deep in the earth they're part of the landscape. *Yes, here*: a half-drowned boy could be watching them all, gripping the wheel, laughing upside down, rolling in the rusted Roadster, blue ghost of himself, alive and not alive, caught in the place between, unwilling to speak as humans speak, wanting only to laugh as water laughs spilling down this river.

A small woman in a loose gray coat watches from across the water. *Please.* She touches her chest with one hand. Does she know who he is, how he failed this morning? *How dare you come to me this way?* Her thin coat flaps in the wind, and she slips the hand inside. *To touch me.*

Such tricks in this light, angels everywhere. She begins to walk again, and he breathes. She's quick for one so small—never slips or stumbles. Soon she's gone between trees, nothing special to him, one woman of many.

He speaks to no one, wants to move fast as light, to see as light sees, everywhere, everything. So slow he is, mud and ice, thick and cold, this human body. He feels Griffin now, imagines him close behind: Griffin the betrayed son, Griffin the hunter—no longer a delicate child in purple tights and black cape, Griffin ten years old, swishing through the house, pretending to be Zorro. *No*, he's grown tall and bearded, narrow as a blade, Griffin slashing through these woods, gaining on him with every step—a man dressed in black jeans and green flannel—Griffin long as the blue shadow of a tree, still as a tree if you turn, shadow of the son always close enough to touch the father.

*You can't hide from me.*

He carries a knife to slit flesh, a bone saw, a rifle.

Horrible to remember—patient Griffin so tenderly helping him into the tub this morning, *after*: Kai already gone three hours, Theo limp from searching. Griffin saw his withered father naked—Theo too numb to speak, too cold this day to deny him.

*No phone, no mail.* Lela says, *If you want Griff, you have to send up a flare or a smoke signal.* But he's always there to feed them, Griffin grinning at the door, bringing morels or huckleberries, venison or elk, trout and salmon. He chops a hole in the ice of some lost lake, waits for pike or perch, bass or kokanee. He knows where wild strawberries grow, where two pheasants are hiding.

Griffin the survivor—no longer the fragile child Theo caught in Naomi's closet, the prettier-than-a-girl pretty boy dressed in Naomi's silk, teetering in his mother's high heels. Theo shaved that boy's silky hair so close he left the scalp nicked and bleeding.

*What madness makes a man afraid of his own child?*

Griffin the thief takes Theo's handsaw with a rusted blade and returns it three months later, clean and sharp, with a curved handle he's carved of cherrywood, sanded and burnished smooth, night after night, as if feeling his father's grip, finding his imprint deep in the grain, learning to love with rasp and blade, steel wool, sandpaper, oil.

Merciful Griffin—no longer the skittery, scared runaway, fifteen years old, arrested in Missoula and returned home nineteen pounds lighter than the night he fled, violet scar looping his neck, leaking wound exposing his belly. That boy refused to sleep in his father's house, slept instead in the silver trailer by the river. *A thousand and one nights.* And every night his mother walked down to the river at dusk to sleep in the trailer beside him.

He's fifty-two years old now, lives alone on Ruby Mountain. Seeks no comfort for himself, offers up his own body. Griffin the fire-cutter believes the blind do lead the blind, and the touch of the burned man cools the pain of others. He's always the one to come—to wash the wound—to splint, to bandage. Griffin heals the crazy horse addicted to locoweed, brushes her dusty coat, shares his apple. *All life is love.* So he teaches. He feeds the little finch, the almost featherless one tossed down in a storm or pushed from the nest by hungry siblings. The bird can't live—he knows this—but he'll feed it six times before he returns the body to the forest. *Here on earth, love is the miracle.*

Griffin the believer drives all night—Montana to Seattle— to sit by the bed where Christine's wild son, his nephew Tulanie Rey, lies unconsciously broken, struck by a car while riding his bicycle. *My peace is my gift.* The boy's been airlifted to Harborview—as if some wizard of a doctor might lay hands on his spine and restore his senses. Griffin knows what it means to be torn open. He sleeps in the chair night after night because Tulanie might wake in the dark and be afraid of blinking lights and beeping monitors, robots roaming the hall, nurses changing shape, becoming ghosts or angels.

Griffin appears before you know you need him. He helps Roy repair the roof, or widen the doors for Tulanie's wheelchair. Griffin guides Angie's misbegotten students into the woods. They're the battered and the bad, the unloved, the unruly. He shows them where to dig, kneels with them to plant their seedlings. *Such bliss!* Whoops become murmurs here, the children quiet at last, in love with their little trees, softly patting damp earth around them.

Griffin the savior finds a gull with a broken wing, a bloody cat with a severed tail. He sits with the wild dog in the ditch, waits with him here—knows he can't lift the coyote and carry him home, can't kiss or bind, can't repair the crushed pelvis. Yes, he should use the rock or the rifle—but he won't because the animal's yellow eyes are too bright, and the little dog's front paws stretch toward him.

*Now, even now, if it be your will, you might save me.*

This morning, Griffin eased Theo into the tepid water of the tub—warm, but not too warm. Hot is dangerous.

*Keep your hands out, Dad.* So softly he spoke, so kind, so terrible. Slowly the brittle skin warmed, slowly blood pulsed back to the surface. *Please,* Theo said, and Griffin left the room, but stood outside the door, listening.

Pitiful old man, rag of skin, sticks trembling. Easy to forgive the one who comes to this, the father who becomes nothing. He might be any old man, any sad, suffering creature.

Now, *yes,* even now, at this late, impossible hour, the son follows in his father's tracks, hoping for Theo to turn, to waver, to wait, to want him. No. Theo imagines the gun raised. If he stops, if he dares to look behind, will Griffin shoot between the eyes—or will the son only wound the old man, taking one small piece at a time: the hand that struck, the mouth that refused to kiss, the knee that pinned him?

Griffin does not hesitate or hurry. He will follow his father through these woods, along this river, from twilight to dusk to early darkness.

*What is love?*

Long shadows falling on blue snow, retreating light, this moment.

# 15

## SURVIVORS

She's already sorry. Wants to unmake the bed, leave the heap of clothes filthy. Wants to lie down where he lay, safe in the shape of him, deep in his body, not like a mother at all, only her child's child. *I could sleep, I could die—till you come home.* Everywhere miracles. Isn't she proof? Born too soon: three pounds, three ounces. *So frail!* Even her mother didn't believe. *So much blood I thought I'd died with you.* She had nothing to give. *Sixty-two hours before you ate, an eyedropper full of milk and sugar. You'd lost nine ounces! From where? I said. There's nothing left of her. Eleven days before you cried. Five weeks before they let me hold you.*

White scilla bloomed wild in the woods, a thousand tiny stars bursting. Ten weeks old and still so fragile: Lela Mikaela Hayes, six pounds, two ounces. Her father carried her beneath his coat. *Along the path, to the river.* So he says, so she believes she remembers—her father kneeling in the dirt to show her a cluster of white blossoms—the smell of him, pine and juniper—the sound of his muffled voice, a song to soothe her—the low vibration of him, one last word rising from his ribs, moving through her—and then only birds, only water over stones riffling.

Now they save babies who weigh less than a pound. And why not? Bears come into the world smaller than this, deaf and blind while their mothers are sleeping. *What more evidence do you need?* Violet pansies bloom under snow. The cold fails to kill, the weight of snow does not crush them.

Last June, ten-year-old Daisy Perkins pulled her cousin Ruth from the river. Four hours since the child slipped between the rails of the fence, followed a blue butterfly into the woods, skidded down the steep gully. Hope at dusk rising and falling. Ruth Laravee might be asleep in the tall grass—might be afraid and hiding. Pretty little Ruth might be in a stranger's car, two hundred miles gone, dressed in dirty bad boy clothes, red hair snipped short, face smudged to hide her freckles.

*No.* Daisy who blamed herself, who promised to watch her favorite cousin, found two-year-old Ruth floating face-down in the water. Nobody else in sight. Nobody there to witness. Only the voice inside: *Call for help. Find your father.* And then another voice: *Only you. You do it.* Daisy yanked Ruth up by her ankles, slapped her back five times. *I don't remember.* But the marks of her hands blazed bright on Ruth's cold skin, so she must have hit hard enough to leave them.

Daisy does remember water spurting from her cousin's mouth, Ruth's face red with rage, that wild cry bursting out of her.

You can say it's not true.

But it is true.

It did happen.

And the little girl lived like other little girls—Lela saw her on television the next day, legs strong enough to walk, words spilling—Ruth Laravee born again, undamaged.

*Cold water,* her doctors said, a kind of human hibernation, everything slow enough not to die, cool blood calming the heart, chilled cells held in stasis.

*Even now, you could be.*

Joseph Trujillo leaped from the West Seattle Bridge and lived though his neck was broken. *Snapped three times,* Tulanie said. *Should have drowned, but walked out of here.*

Tulanie flew from his bike one summer day—was lifted up into the trembling light and slammed down hard on the pavement. *Still fast,* he says. *In my wheelchair.*

Who decides?

Last November, one-legged Willis Brodie pulled 216-pound Vincent Flute out the window of his rolled truck as the battery sparked and gas trickled, dragged him up the steep bank seconds before flames exploded. *I don't know how. I can't explain it.* The photograph of Willis Brodie filled the front page of the paper, left pantleg split to the knee to expose his prosthesis. Seventy-three years old, this savior. Maybe one of them will come—the crippled man or the man not on fire. *Maybe their crazy faith will call you up—maybe their eyes will see you.*

Lela remembers the mild August day rescuers pulled Evan Biel from a crevasse on Sperry Glacier. Barely fourteen inches wide that crack in ice, ice walls slick as glass, ice rain raining. Two men climbed down sixty-five feet to find Evan wedged in ice, still alive, softly moaning. His warm body had melted the ice, but now it froze hard around him, locking his head in place, gripping one twisted leg, holding his hip and shoulders.

The men chipped him free, whispering the whole time, like fathers, like brothers. *Don't be afraid. We're here. We love you.*

Why did Evan Biel stop believing? Even in the helicopter, paramedics swore they heard his heart flutter.

*Too cold*, Doctor Kober said. Lela was there that day, working at the hospital, and she remembered Evan, a boy she liked who never noticed her in high school. They kept him on a respirator all night. Tried all night to warm him. *Where are you?* His mother couldn't make him rise. His wife Nicole couldn't tempt him. *Let me be.* Brain too numb to spark, too many bones broken. *Please.* Words formed in Nicole's mind. *Let me go. I'm so tired.*

Nobody knows why. Only the dead can explain it.

Last Sunday, the beautiful woman on TV, the soldier home from Iraq with shrapnel still deep in her brain, said doctors gave her one chance in a hundred to wake, one in a thousand to do more than bob and babble. And here she was, radiantly amazed, smiling sweetly.

*Somebody had to be the one*, she said. *Why couldn't I do it?*

In a tent, in a field hospital outside Baghdad, Jodee Beddia's surgeon cut a piece of bone from her skull so her swelling brain wouldn't kill her. *Sewed it inside my abdomen*, she said. *To keep the bone alive. So nobody would lose it.* Jodee Beddia flew home in a coma.

Now the bone is back in her head—she's stapled and sutured. *Pain, yes, always. Like light*, she says, *cutting through me.*

She traces a line from between her eyes, up over the crown, through both temples. *Sometimes a jolt,* she says. *One more explosion.* Her finger moves down the stem. She smiles. *It's only pain, a friend if you call it that, not so bad to be awake, alive today to feel it.*

One bright day last winter, thirteen-year-old Rosanna Rios arrived at the hospital in time to give her heart and lungs—liver, spleen, pancreas, kidneys. In time to surrender her perfectly clear corneas and twenty-six inches of unscarred skin to save the lives, restore the sight, heal the burns of seven others.

Why should a sixty-nine-year-old man receive the heart of a child?

*Your mercy spills, or doesn't.*

One sobbing child pulled from a neighbor's well, one drowned in his mother's bathtub.

*You give us life to lose.*

One boy hiding under the road, playing a game, trapped in a culvert.

*You offer terrible grace.*

One bruised baby found in a field of tall grass, alive and unafraid after a tornado, this one of nine hundred lifted up and set down, everything destroyed around her.

Dizzy on the stairs—Lela's up and down again, looking for one last thing—a sock, a bandanna—something she failed to wash, something still precious. *I could fall. I could die. Bloom as my mother bloomed. Be gone. Be done. Be with you.*

She clutches a faded t-shirt, a soft blue rag with a dozen holes and ripped collar—his favorite, the one she threatened to toss—now washed clean like all the others—no sweat, no blood—only the faintest trace of him lingering beneath the sting of detergent.

*I forbid you.*

She wants to rock in Kai's bed, deep in the curve of him, down in his cradle—wants to rock all night, night after night, wants it to be night always, *rock me unto death*, yes, as if in water. *You'll freeze.* Why did her father go out in the cold when it took Griff three hours to warm him? *Go then.* Why tempt God? So cold the wind at the door, so fierce the last light blazing. She wants Theo home again, to fling hope against his doubt, not to know what she's known all day even as she cooked and scrubbed, stripped the bed, rolled pairs of socks so carefully together.

*Do the living feel our faith? Will your heart stop if I stop believing?*

One chickadee comes to the feeder. Even now, so close to twilight! Less than half an ounce of feather and hollow bone, ten drops of blood, heart smaller than a fingernail—yet she survives all night, every night, all winter.

*Why not you?*

Five-year-old Iris disappeared at noon one hot day, stayed gone all night through the summer storm, gone all night in the cold rain. Sun-scorched little Iris didn't freeze in the rain, didn't drown in a ditch, didn't crawl in a culvert. Dugan kept her safe in the dark, dry in his dog house. Huge and warm, enormously kind, Dugan her friend, grateful to have her.

Griffin came home alive after eight months—belly cut, teeth broken—not like her brother at all—blistered skin scratched raw—more like a starved animal. Nobody ever explained. *Your brother was dead, and now has come back to us.* She remembers that weird burned smell, Griff's horrible breath for weeks after.

*Even now.*

Kai could be outside looking in, too cold to knock, too blue to see, too numb to call her.

Once upon a time, so long ago, one terrible November night, she locked him out. She did this. Six years old, her only one, her love, her child. *Hush little baby.* The one she sang to sleep. *Don't say a word.* Halloween ten days gone, snow on the ground, Kai outside alone wearing nothing but blue socks and red pajamas. How long did she let him shiver?

Long enough to wipe spit peas from the floor, mop spilled milk, change the tablecloth.

He'd mashed the peas flat on his plate, refused to eat them. *Such will!* She snatched the potatoes he loved, the drumstick he wanted. Said he could have them back when he ate the peas. *Every last one of them.*

*So hungry!*

He wanted to tear her chicken wing from the bone, break the bone, suck the marrow—wanted to steal the bright green bowl full of creamy white whipped potatoes. He gripped the spoon, impolite, fingers forward—raised the spoon to his mouth, closed his eyes to eat, whole body trembling. Even the smell, so terrible, stronger with his eyes closed—*be quick, be done*—he slipped the sticky peas into his mouth, dropped the spoon, tried to swallow—reached for the milk to wash them down, but she grabbed that too. *No, chew them.*

He tried—he did—but couldn't do it. Spat the peas instead, spewed them across the table, splattered the yellow cloth, spattered his mother. She dumped the milk over his head. *Crazy,* she thought even as she watched her bad self do this. He flung the plate to the floor, and together they watched peas fly, china shatter.

Both of them wailing now, so loud she thought Mrs. Novak next door must hear them. Delores Novak, crazy herself— Lela hoped that eighty-five-year-old, ninety-eight-pound whirling dervish would burst through the door and save them.

Did she grab his arm, twist hard, hurt him? She was twice his size, but he had that terrible boy strength, *just like your father*, was twisting his own arm to break the bone or break free of her. She heard weird little yipping sounds, herself or him, she can't remember, saw him biting his own hand, *to keep from biting me*, biting so hard he pierced skin, and she let him go, smacked his head hard, smacked hard again to stop him.

He stared at her, amazed, spat a word she couldn't hear, and bolted. She tried to catch, but oh, he was quick and small, scared and furious, buzzing from the blows, crazy as she was. He was out the door, slipping free, slamming the door behind him.

*Fine*, she said out loud, and locked it.

*Just for a minute.*

Just long enough to clean this mess, stop gasping.

She swept the shattered china from the floor, wiped the peas and milk, put the food away. *No evidence.*

*How long?*

She stuffed the dirty tablecloth in the wash, laid a clean one on the table.

*Where are you?*

Forgot how cold it was outside, the boy in red pajamas.

Did she see him at the window—does she see him now?

Blue face pressed to glass, skin stretched tight, a boy's starved face, so hungry all day, so much smaller than he was this morning.

*How many minutes?*

*Are those your fingerprints on the pane? Is that you knocking?*

She doesn't know, she can't be sure how long she left him out there.

Nobody now, no fingers, no face, no fists hammering.

She opened the door wide and called him. Whirling snow, wind answered. She ran out in the cold without her coat, circled the house, thinking he must be here, crouched in the bushes hiding. *So cold!* She knew now how cold he was. She thought she'd find him under the sharp juniper, knees tucked tight to his thin chest, *hush little baby*, rocking himself to sleep, *forever and ever.*

Never so afraid, never so sorry.

She's seen the signs everywhere: runaways, throwaways, un-loved, unlucky—scarred, tattooed, cut, stolen—thrown from windows, shaken half to death, burned, buried—left for dead but not dead, too afraid to cry, somewhere still waiting.

She's blamed the mothers of the lost, cursed the fathers who abandoned.

*Please, just this once—I won't, I'll never.*

She ran house to house thinking someone must have seen, hoping some kind stranger had him. She imagined him asleep on a neighbor's couch, dressed in some other little boy's soft, warm flannel pajamas.

She remembers a row of jack-o'-lanterns grinning in the dark, old men now, burned lips, heads collapsing. She met a scarecrow nailed to a pole, arms flapping in the wind, sleeves empty. She heard tiny ghosts fluttering in bare branches, a tree full of whispering rags, little heads stuffed, bodies blowing.

She found a stunted snowman with a deer's antlers, pitted and pocked by last week's rain, one side washed away, one antler still high on his head, one a crippled limb dangling. She stood alone in the dark with the battered snowman, one more little boy lost, one more frozen child. Half-frozen herself, listening to ghosts in the wind, hoping the scarecrow would lift one limp arm, point the way, and save her.

And she was saved. *Just this once.*

Eleven years later she's pulling on boots and gloves, slipping into her down jacket. She knows now where to go, what to do, how to love him.

## 16

## Unforgiven

*Lullaby for Lela*

How can you forgive if she never says she's sorry?
Eleven years since Mother locked you out, and even
now you wonder why you spat the peas, why she slapped
you—why you ran out in the snow wearing only red pajamas.

Does she remember your fists pounding at the door, your
head banging on the window? You pressed your face to cold
glass, flattened your lips and nose, tried to scare her. Did your
mother see you dancing in the dark? *So cold in my wet socks!*

Does she know now, does she imagine?

You ran away from a stuffed man in a knit cap and black
jacket. His head was the skull of a goat, too small for him,
somebody else's head, found in a ditch, dug from a field. You
saw his long white nose, the buds of little horns protruding.
He wore leather boots laced high, spiked for climbing trees
or mountains. He wanted to kill you with his glittering axe,
a child's toy wrapped in foil. Flickering lights made him ap-

pear and disappear, lurch and lunge, alive in light, withered in shadow.

An eight-foot-tall man made of snow saved you. He seemed very kind, eye holes filled with dark fruit, pecked by birds, but not stolen. *Don't be afraid. Nobody's real.* One arm was the blade of a saw, the other a broken paddle.

Your mother found you hours later, safe in Tulanie's bed, curled up close with your cousin. *Let them sleep,* Aunt Christine said. *I'll bring him in the morning.*

You never spoke of it—then, or after. Never spat peas, never made your mother smack you. You heard her whisper in the dark hallway. *So scared, so sorry.* Why didn't she come back into Tulanie's room, scoop you from the bed, say the words out loud, both at once, you two, together? You could have opened your eyes and gone home. *Let them sleep.* You refused to be the first, refused to cry out to her. Yes, let her go. Let Mother lie in her own bed, awake all night, alone, throbbing.

You remember holding Iris—another night, a perfect night, not so long after—you and Tulanie lying on the floor, Iris crawling back and forth over your bellies. Almost two and just washed, Iris flushed pink as the pink inside poppies. She howled when Christine tried to take her away—so you carried her down the hall, you sat in the chair, you sang a love song lullaby, a song your mother sang to you, *hush little baby,* and you did forgive, and you do forgive, *don't you cry,* and you both fell asleep as you rocked her.

PART FOUR

# 17

## The Companionship of Stone

Almost twilight and Daniel Sidoti still believes he might find the missing boy and pull him from the river. Kai Dionne, seventeen years old, almost a man, six feet tall, but only 146 pounds, a child willing to die to save an animal. *Where are you?* So long ago it seems: gold light spilled through trees, morning light diffused by thin fog, illuminating frost on fine needles. Ice popped as sun sparked, fractures radiating from the hole where Kai leaped to save the dog and both plunged, swept under. *Talia!* The first cracks split wide and new ones fissured, a tremor river to root, water breaking ice, trees trembling. Talia returned to shore hours later, eyes dull, heart silent.

*Anything is possible.* Even now Daniel keeps his faith. Wasn't he found alive after nineteen hours? A heap of rags on the road. *Is this a man?* He thought he'd died there.

All day he's followed the quick boy, the one who looks like Kai Dionne, but isn't. No, only his frail ghost, six inches shorter, thirty pounds lighter than Kai, blond hair almost white, fine as a baby's. This one is sticks and leaves, faded camouflage—one of twenty homeless kids, a pack of strays moving fast downriver.

At dawn, firefighters bounded across snow, thirteen believers towing a sled built to glide on ice or float on water. They'd saved an elk last week, a black Labrador in December.

One hawk circling high, five crows watching.

Women singing Kai's name.

Then ice broke and sun shattered, a bone-popping shiver in the skull, sound and light all one, water rushing.

Every child he saw made Daniel's heart stutter. They kept taking shape between trees, wisps of fog rising to reveal one more, fluttering through brush, small and human.

*We die every night, wake every morning.*

Feral dogs tore in and out of the woods, bringing rags and broken birds, stuffed toys, hoof and hair, gifts for the children. The boy in camouflage raised one bare hand, *Yes, I know*, a sign to Daniel. Blue veins, thin skin, *Here I am*, fingers moving. He spoke to one dog, and Tejano came, something filthy in his mouth, long dark tail wagging.

Hours later, the boy appeared alone, high on a ridge, the sky clear, bright blue, wind whipping fine snow, the delicate child whirling out of it, *no, not me*, only light in snow, particles of boy disappearing. The river here ran fast and narrow, breaking brittle ice from shore, pulling snared limbs down its open channel.

Half a mile downstream, the child cut back to climb a bare willow, perch still as an owl and that silent, waiting for the lost boy to drift by or fly under.

*Is this love?*

He fell from the sky, ten feet in front of Daniel.

Only once did the child linger long enough for Daniel to see skin stretched tight, fine bones of the face, skull of a little fox, green bruise above the right eyebrow. He smelled dirt and hair, burning leaves, a pile of feathers. Dared to imagine touching the boy's rib, feeling the wild flutter, *whoosh* of blood in the vein, heart's murmur.

Last night Daniel's daughters slipped down the long hall and into the living room—a game they loved, stealing music. Clare covered his eyes with her cool hands. Nora couldn't stop giggling. They wanted to play a song Angie Dionne had taught them.

*Then to bed, we promise.*

Such a sweet lie!

They did play, Clare's notes precise and perfect, clear in her mind, memorized just today, *easy to follow*—Nora's a tumbling riff, above and then below, birds answering birds, stones talking to the river. She played by running side to side, not reading notes, *not remembering*, only listening to wood and wire, feeling hammers strike, *inside*, letting sound spill through her. Six years old! *A genius*, Angie says—and Daniel says, *Don't tell her.*

Nora hasn't learned what can't be done, what isn't possible. She thinks anyone can play. *Even you, Daddy.* She can't explain how. *Don't you hear? Watch me.*

The homeless boy had stuffed his pants with old newspaper. Useless words, but warm in their way, crumpled against him. He pulled a piece out for Daniel to see, pretended to read, then let the wind take it.

*Peter Fleury!* The child who calls himself No, who eats dirt and leaves to fill his stomach, who hears bones dissolve and blood dividing—this motherless boy whispered his name, his real name—he didn't know why until he bolted into the woods and heard the man cry out.

*Peter!*

When the cinnamon bear staggers from her den in early spring, the marks she leaves in mud look almost human. She stands on her hind legs and walks this way to make him want, to fool him. *You could be mine.* She's all hunger. *I could pull you close, smother you in my thick fur, love you this way.*

Mother had a fur coat, fake fur sewn in long pelts to look real. Dark as mink, thick as otter. Peter Fleury loved that coat, small body warm inside it. Loved to woof and whine, lunge and leap, chase his little brother down the stairs, growling.

Alone, in the closet, he turned the coat outside in. Wore it naked. How did she know? *Don't you dare. Don't you ever.* She gave his bike to little Nick. *Because you don't deserve. Because you don't respect me.*

*No.*

Today, Peter Fleury risked his life for no good reason. Where water churned with green silt and broken ice, the boy danced stone to stone to cross the river. Tempting God. *Throw me down. Pull me under.*

He looked back and saw the man on the other side, denying him now, afraid to follow.

*Anyone can die anytime.*

The night Daniel Sidoti spun on Marias Pass, the deer he'd swerved to miss leaped free and vanished. So beautiful to know, the animal alive, everything as it was, everyone safe here. He steered into the spin, but kept spinning. *I'm the one.* He tapped the brakes twice, felt a glaze of ice beneath snow, tires skidding. *My life for yours.* The clarity of the words, the weird peace, the deer's eyes, the memory of them, the long dark space beyond the beams of his headlights, a flurry of light snow— everything here, now, amazed him.

He climbed with numb hands and fractured pelvis. *Because I didn't know. Torn,* I thought, *bruised, not broken.* Days later, in the hospital, he saw how horrible he was—fingers black, face bandaged—he couldn't turn in bed, couldn't lift a cup of water, couldn't raise his head or curl his toes without pain searing through his pelvis.

He couldn't explain how he'd climbed, what he believed, why he continued. Cloud, tree, snow, moon: everything watching. *This is why.* Snow falling on snow. Snow melting on eyelid. Skin no longer warm, *no longer mine,* no longer human.

The moon drifted behind clouds, hiding its face, but filling the sky with rings of light. *I will not leave you comfortless.*

He crawled ten feet at a time, saw one tree taller than the rest, more courteous or kind, heavy with snow, bending toward him. *So patient!* Lower limbs pulled down by snow took root in earth not quite frozen. Soft in its way, this dark earth, warm enough beneath snow for life to begin. *Even as you die here.*

Two hours gone since Peter Fleury lost Daniel. The sky glows, not the sun dropping behind western hills, but the reflection of light across the valley: pink snow on high peaks, a thin line of coral clouds, gold edges. A brilliant lie, promising light and day, *hope*, ten more hours to search, pale sky tinged turquoise. *No.* Already the woods are dark, trees blurred, everything shifting shape, limbs becoming birds, stones becoming fox and rabbit. Darkness doesn't fall: it rises. Comes from dark earth. Swallows.

The ice here looks thin as a pane of glass, but clouded. He can't see through. In this light, in this space between day and dark, air and water, a boy trapped beneath ice could press his body against the pane and still be unknown, only the shape of a boy—nothing, no one—shadow of a tree submerged, smooth green stones deep in the riverbed.

The moon floats high, a white crescent. Here is the truth: he has half an hour of fading light. *To love or fail.* He'll need the eyes of the owl, wide as human eyes, and a hundred times more sensitive.

*whoo – whoo – whoo*

*wowhua   ow – ow – owhua*

The bird speaks. Somewhere far away a dog answers, his voice tremulous as the owl's, three tones at once from his throat rising. *Tejano?* His howl at dusk is hope and the lack of it, something found, *heap of rags*, something possible: Peter or Kai, one lost child recovered.

Daniel no longer knows which boy he hopes to find.

*Persistence is love.*

He keeps moving.


Peter Fleury whispers to the missing boy, his lost self, his twin, his double, *my shadow drowned—me, us, we might be whole if I can find you.* So many places for a body to hide. All day, Peter Fleury has wondered what his own body might choose if he were the one drowned or not drowned, if he plunged after the dog he loved and felt hair in his hands, Tejano's body pulled away from him.

Fearless, he is, deaf to reason. Tejano could have been the one. Peter would have tried to save him. *Died with you today. Not been sorry.*

When Peter crossed the river, stone to slick stone, he felt how easy it would be to slip, *so fast,* to surrender. *Who can say when? Who deserves mercy?* He learned how far the man wouldn't come, whose child he would refuse to follow.

He circled back to find Tejano, to see Iris again, Neville and Trina—to toss snowballs to the dog. To pretend, to imagine. A day like any other day. *Nobody gone. Nothing missing.* Tejano knocked him to the ground, forty pounds flying.

He yipped to make Peter follow, and together these two climbed a steep slope.

Three hawks whirled high above, watching humans move along the water's edge, so small and slow, voices muted.

Tejano caught a scent deep in the woods, flash of red fox, his wild brother. *Such joy to love!* Tejano burst down the ravine through brush and bramble. Too crazy to catch. Too quick to follow.

Lost again, more than an hour, but Peter hears him now, somewhere downstream, yipping and wailing. He could be ten dogs, a pack of wolves, coyotes crying to the night, owls waking.

Everybody wants to be found.

*Even you Tejano.*

One dark day last December, Peter walked out along the tracks, saw five mule deer and nine whitetails, three spotted horses with long hair, six feral cats, two tame rabbits. *Why can't I be one?*

He watched humans inside their shacks and trailers, warm no matter how poor, safe in their squares of light, loved by some blind dog, sniffed and known by some other creature.

*I'll die if you don't come. Die if you don't touch me.*

> *wof – wof – woo*
>
> *oo' koo – koo – koo*

He didn't know who he meant until the birds called him.

> *whoo – oo – who*
>
> *ooah – woo*

A whole coop of white rock doves.

> *ooah – woo – woo – woo*

They wanted him to come

> *whooooooooo  ooooooooh*

to slip inside

> *who – koo – koo – koo*

They weren't afraid. He smelled the same, or worse, dirtier than they were.

> *oo – oo – whoo*

Their bodies amazed him. *So warm! So much warmer than I am.*

Filthy, yes, shit and feathers. He scraped a place clean in the dirt, curled into it. Any moment the sad, sunken man in the trailer—the thin man with slack belly—might bolt into the yard, waving his shotgun. Any moment, the bent, brittle wife might let the snapping dogs loose. Let them come, let them do it.

*whoo – oo – whoo*

He slept as birds spoke, their songs his breath, their blood his body.

*ow – ow – owhua*
Tejano wailing
*whoo – hoo – hoo*
the owl answering

A thin sheen of water on ice mirrors the fading sky, silvery blue, soft lavender. *Show me where!* The night Daniel skidded off Marias Pass seven mountain goats appeared, white in the white world. *To follow or lead me.* He couldn't die with them watching.

At dawn sun sheared off snow, blinded and scorched him. A mouthful shrank to a single drop and left him limp, colder than he was in the night, face burned, core quivering. He prayed for the night to come again—for sleep, for silence, for the goats to turn away long enough to let him die, cover him with snow, or open him fast, hooves flashing. He heard the roar of water under ice, a river deep in the ravine—but in his thirst, its voice thunderous. He should have climbed down, not up, died last night at the river's edge, not thirsty.

All day the river spoke: *I could have spared you.*

Birds filled the sky, too many to know or number, wings and tails catching light: pale pink, spark of silver. A rippling flock with one voice, each bird and all birds rising and falling, wings beating fast, then pulled tight, bodies gliding. *So close they dared to come!* A great warm wind of bird flying through, flying out of him. *Now you know!* They took his breath. He rose with them. *Yes:* the man who was not a man saw a bag of sticks and bones far below him.

Twilight: the terrible sun gone. Now the dark could hide, the cold take him. He thought the moon must rise, but it didn't, and he crawled in absolute darkness. Not to survive, not to be delivered. Only to move closer to the road, to be found after. So Denise would know. So Clare and Nora wouldn't say, *Yes, we understand Daddy's dead, but where is he?*

He believed he could smell asphalt and tar, cold pavement beneath snow, fumes lingering. He felt the companionship of stone, trees heavy with snow bending toward him. He would die or not die, and these things would be as they were now: everywhere touching him. He lay on his back watching stars appear, one by one until the black sky burst, the whole universe just now exploding.

He tried to curl into himself one last time, but pain locked his spine and pelvis, pinned him flat on his back, left him shaking. He understood he couldn't do this small thing, couldn't turn on his side and pull his knees to his chest—could only lie as he was, not moving. The loss of himself amazed him. He was not brave or kind or stupid. Not guilty or good. Not strong. Not tender. These words meant nothing now in the cold with only trees and stars to witness.

He saw the lights of a distant car, winding up the road, moving toward him. The ones inside would see or not see, recognize his human shape and stop—or whisper, *What was that?*, and drive past him.

There was nothing on earth to want. Everything was here: the merciful cold, stones beneath snow, trees breathing into the night, his quiet companions. He was glad he couldn't move, couldn't hide his face from stars, couldn't not be seen by stars, a storm of stars, more stars than he'd ever dreamed, whirling above, whirling toward him.

Tejano runs up and down the shore, silent now, bounding toward Peter—but reeling before the boy can touch, sprinting back to the place where the river has cut a cave under the bank, left long roots dangling. A secret place: tangle of root snagging cans and rags, the torn limbs of other trees, rusted tin, plastic bottles.

*Yes, here.* Something caught and cradled, snared inside, rocked by water. This is what Tejano wants, what keeps him running in circles, impatient for the boy to come, still spinning after all these hours.

Peter knows he could find anything: a deer broken through ice and trapped, dead three days, slowly swelling—a coat torn free, a body missing—or only a bag of garbage snared, something raw and rotten inside, its smell making Tejano wild.

Last week the dog dug Rikki out of the snow, his favorite motherless girl dreaming herself dead, so peaceful.

*Please, leave me.* Rikki loved the dream, her body safe inside it.

Peter hopes for the man to appear, dark from dark woods, to speak his name. *Now, before I see.* To stand beside, to see with him.

# 18

## Birdsong Under Water

All day Tulanie's stayed trapped in the attic—window open wide, wind blowing—praying for the pigeon to die, or rise up and leave him. She did go. He must have closed his eyes too long. Now she lies limp on the floor. *Sticks and feathers.*

Three times today he's drifted down deep enough to hear Talia bounding up the stairs, *alive,* proving his father wrong, bringing Kai with her. All day he's hoped: *Please, someone, any-one—tie me to a sled, drag me to the river.*

He smells his mother's skin on sheets and pillows. They've been washed thirty times in five years. But she remains. *Whisper me to sleep, kiss and vanish.* He wants Iris to come, *now,* this moment—strip the sheets, bleach or burn them.

In late afternoon, gold dust swirled in a slant of light, and Dorrie Esteban appeared as light in light, cradling the pigeon. *So beautiful, you are.* The bird who refused to die trembled, radiant in her body: feathers alive with light, throat shimmering. If he'd tried to touch, if he'd crawled, if he'd dragged his crippled self across the floor, his cold hand would have passed in and out of light and straight through them.

Elia Esteban sat perched in the open window, bones hollow as a bird's, black hair soft as feathers.

*You know it's true.*

Kai gone—Dorrie, Elia.

*You can't touch.*

*No matter how fast you fly.*

*You can't save us.*

*Tulanie?*

Yes, at last, his name called, a word outside himself, not just blood pounding. He knows who before he sees—not Dorrie, not Iris—Lela climbing the stairs, soft step, soft breathing, *only you*, a voice he heard in the womb, a hand he felt on his head so long ago, *touch me now*, when he was safe inside his mother.

*Let it be.*

He wants Lela to speak the truth. *Say it fast. Please. Tell me.*

*Shush. It's okay. We don't know yet.*

Twilight: the sky still blue, deep blue, the day done, *we do know*, the bird dead, faint glow of rose and green behind bare maples, *touch me*, Mother's smell, *on my skin*, Dorrie whispering, *you can't touch*, Elia flying out the window.

Lela moves to close it. Hours too late.

*Please. Leave the window open.*

*You're cold, Tulanie.*

*Yes. I want to be.*

She lies down close beside him, *beautiful boy*, such strange peace to touch: shoulders, ribs, hands, pelvis—not as tall as Kai, but five inches longer than she is—*Tulanie Rey, almost my own*, her sister's child, born nine days before Kai, cousins closer than brothers.

*He loved you before you were born. No one else like you—no one, ever. I felt him leap in me every time I kissed your mother. You jumped and kicked, both inside, so joyful!*

*We couldn't wait!*

*To be together.*

*We heard you laugh!*

*You can't remember that.*

*We do remember. You sounded like birds.*

*Loons!*

*Laughing underwater.*


Tim Dionne crouches at the river's edge, listening to water under ice, *whoosh* and crackle, limbs snapping in the cold,

> *hoo – coo – coo – quoo*
> *hoo – coo – coo – quoo*
> owls waking.

All day he's willed himself to believe, even when he saw Roy with Talia in his arms, staggering in the snow, drenched by the dog, shivering hard, not wailing. He wouldn't put her down. *No.* He refused to rest. He wanted to get Talia to the truck, wrap her in a blanket. He wouldn't take a swallow from Tim's flask, wouldn't sit in the truck and blast the heater. *No.* He changed his gloves and jacket, called Tulanie Rey. Called Lela. What could he say?

*The crows found her.*

Crazy, all of them. Waiting for signs: a slant of light, a bird, an animal. This morning Tim Dionne followed a whitetail doe more than a mile into the woods—because she appeared at the edge of the river, because she lowered her head to drink and saw him, and wasn't afraid and drank while he watched and let the sun strike her.

*You might be spared!*

Even now.

*If you believe, if you follow.*

He lost her an hour later. The doe hid her tracks in the tracks of others—dogs and deer, bobcat, human.

*You don't know who I am. You don't love me.*

In late afternoon, he drove fifteen miles to his own house—to be sure Juliana and Roxie were safe and warm, home from school. He couldn't go inside. They'd kiss. They'd touch him. He called Angie from his cell phone. *Come to the window. I'm across the street. I need to see you.* She pressed one hand to the glass, and he whispered, *Do they know? Did you tell them?*

Twice he drove past Lela's house, thinking if he could go home tonight—if this were home—Kai would be there.

*But only if Roxie and Juliana never are.*

*Only if Angie never loves you.*

The ice speaks.

*What you want and what is both destroy you.*

He remembers now walking out on the ice of the reservoir with his brother thirty-five years ago—a January morning so cold he felt his breath stop in his throat, lungs burning. Vale wasn't cold. *No, never.* He unzipped his coat and danced across the ice to prove it. Whooped and hollered, pulled his gloves off, sent his red flame of scarf flying.

Nothing hurt, nothing scared him.

The ice moaned, a living thing. *Growing*, Vale said. *Safe— that's when you hear it.* The ice creaked and cried, its voice a low growl, its echo through trees and stone rumbling.

Vale pulled Tim close to spin and twirl. *The river's never safe. One minute you're waltzing on ice and the next you're walking on water.*

They skidded halfway across the reservoir before Vale took the hatchet from his belt. *I'll show you.* Two inches, three—Vale kept chopping. *Perfectly safe. See how thick?* Tim felt foolish then: little boy, shivering child. Almost four inches down before Vale broke through and they saw not water, but air—twenty-five feet of air beneath them—then another layer of ice, the reservoir drained after the first freeze, and frozen again in a second layer. Below that, three hundred feet of black water.

*Dead men walking.* Not safe, not anywhere. They'd fall like stones.

Sun burned through clouds and ice groaned, plates shifting. They spread their bodies wide on the ice. *Make yourself an angel*, Vale said, his voice soft, just this once serious.

Angels, *yes*, blessed that day. They crawled inch by inch back to shore on their bellies. *Don't you ever tell. Dad would skin me.*

He remembers how cold they were, faces raw, muscles cramping, Vale's red scarf lost on the ice, Vale's red scarf fluttering.

Nineteen years later Vale Dionne slipped on the ice outside his apartment, bled into his brain, lay on the ice three hours before Mrs. Odegard looked out her window and saw him.

Five months before he learned to walk again, nine before he started talking.

*Scared straight*, he said. Sober all that time. Saved in the hospital.

By spring the next year he was back in bed, liver failing, safe in his parents' house, dying in the room where he'd slept as a child.

*Don't worry, little brother. I'm number five thousand seven hundred twenty-seven for transplant.* A joke, even now.

Tim said, *Take half of mine.* A perfect match, they could be. He imagined a piece of his liver swelling up to full size, growing soft and dark inside his brother. A miracle. *They can, you know—it's possible.* He would have given Vale his left lung, his right kidney. Three pints of blood. *Anything you need.* Anything to save him.

*Tell you what,* Vale said. *There's a twenty in my wallet. Bring me a fifth of Jack. That's what will help. That's what we need here.*

He couldn't explain. *Close the window when you go. I don't like listening to the birds. I just get so tired.*

So hot, too hot already. Tim shut the window tight, never returned that night—or the next day—or the night after. Never bought his brother's whiskey. Stayed gone till Vale was done saying stupid things. *The birds, sweet Jesus, close the window.* Till he was beautiful and still, down deep in a coma, flooded with poison, *ammonia, creatinine,* toxins his body couldn't flush. Mother called. *Come today if you want to see him.*

Tim opened the window wide. *To listen to the birds*, he said.
*I think he's ready.*

He remembers layers of sound
*ooah – woo – woo – woo*
doves under the eaves,
wrens trilling—
a thrush whistling in the woods,
high then low,
a long sweet warble—
Mother whispering, *It's okay*,
a dog in the house next door barking.

He remembers his father pacing the hall, a soft, terrible sound: thump of the cane, left foot dragging. Vireos sang dawn to dusk. Ten thousand songs. Ten thousand questions. He remembers his father slumped in a chair downstairs, gasping for breath, shoulders heaving. And later, *after*, a night of summer rain—rain on the roof—vireos hiding high in dark leaves, sheltered from the storm, still asking—vireos singing all night, his father rocking on the porch, flash and flare of a match, red glow of the cigarette lit, rain on the roof thrumming.

Now, at dusk, thin clouds blow down from the north and a light frazzle of snow begins to fall on ice and melt in water. Two herons rise over the half-frozen river. So cold! *You can't be here.*

But they are here.
They are real.
Silent birds circling in snow.

*Sleep, my love.*
No songs now.
*No need to wake.*
No need to listen.

# 19

## Early Darkness

3 February 2006: 6:30 p.m.

The black bear rises out of a dream—fat moths, ripe berries—but does not open her eyes or turn, only surfaces far enough to pull the two squalling cubs deep into her dark fur, back to her warm nipples. The female cub weighs seven ounces, her brother nine. They fit in the cups of their mother's paws, feel light as birds on the mass of her body.

Last fall she spent five days digging this cave, excavating the earth beneath a fallen cedar. Now the sweet smell of decay fills her. She lined the hole with twigs and grass, leaves and needles, but the floor is cold, the cubs blind and naked.

She gave birth in the bliss of sleep six days ago. She does not count, does not remember, but the shudder of high voices reminds her she's not alone, pierces through dream to warn: *Don't roll, don't crush us.*

The den is small, its opening barely wide enough for her to squeeze through when she was fat and full last October. She hasn't eaten since then, hasn't voided in the den, or pushed her nose outside it. Now she eats what the cubs leave, keeping the cave clean, licking their bare bodies. By early spring, more than a third of her weight will be gone, fat transformed to heat, fuel for bone and milk and muscle.

The cubs cannot hear their own cries or soft trembling murmurs. Deaf now they are, toothless—but they feel their small frames quiver with sound and know how their mother's rough tongue and deep fur and sweet milk soothe them.

They will never understand how miraculous their lives are. For five months they floated free in their mother's womb, clusters of cells, embryos fertilized but not implanted. They didn't attach themselves to the wall of the uterus until their mother was safe and warm in the den, asleep at last, fat enough to survive winter.

They cannot conceive the dangers outside. Cannot imagine cold or snow, thin ice, fast water. A starved grizzly could find them even now, tear through earth, take them from her.

In lush, wet, flowering spring, they'll meet wolves and mountain lions. Skunks, raccoons, moose, martens. Swarms of ticks! Bees, snakes, birds, mosquitoes. They'll smell rabid dogs and terrified humans. Bobcats, voles, porcupines, weasels. They'll eat lilies dug from dark earth and trout pulled from the green river. Climb the straight trunks of ponderosa pine and sway in high branches. They'll bite rocks and chew grass and scavenge the carcass of an elk killed by wolves and left for coyotes and crows, magpies, eagles. One perfect day in late summer, the forty-two-pound cubs will wrestle and roll and tumble together down a slope of fiery shooting stars and deep blue forget-me-nots.

But now the dark den is home, their mother's mysterious body their whole world.

> *hoo – coo – coo – quoo*
> One owl speaks,
> *whoo – whoo – whoo*
> and another answers.

Tejano howls at the birds. Why won't they help him? He bites Peter's sleeve and pulls hard, but the boy refuses to move, to know everything he knows—to touch and free what he's found snared in roots.

Not the body of a deer, not a bag full of garbage.

*It is dark, dark where I'm going.*

Owls hear the dead murmur under water.

*I am not afraid.*

Owls see blond hair float, silky in the current. Bare white hands. One shoe lost, one bare pale foot waving.

> A boy who's almost a man
> *hoo – coo – coo*
> rocking at the river's edge
> *whoo – whoo – whoo*
> long body caught and cradled.

He changes the river's flow. Water touches him and swirls.

Tejano smells the coyote on the ridge, the tired man stumbling through trees upriver. He yelps to tell them where. Sings and wails and shivers.

Daniel Sidoti stoops to pass under a narrow bridge, barely wide enough for one car, wood split, steel corroded. The beam of his headlamp catches snow, illuminates and defines, holds each crystal.

Above the gully, streetlamps shimmer, a weird glow, amber and violet, light diffused by snow, halos of light, color scattered. The edge of town hovers high in the distance, less than a mile from here, but new and strange. Another time. Another world. *Where my daughters live.* Where Clare plays a major trill, and little Nora runs side to side, high then low—Nora, water over stone, ice crackling.

     *owhua – owhua*

     The last voice on earth, Tejano howling.

     Who else is there to trust? Daniel doesn't know if he's heard where the dog's cries begin or only caught their echoes. *Go back. Cross over.* All his senses now befuddled by snow, even the dog's wild voice muted.

     Flakes cluster, six joined to one, big as moths, lightly touching. Their bodies refract light. Obscure trees, bridge, road, water. The beam of the headlamp reveals snow inside of snow. *Now you can die. Now you know nothing.*

     Too cold to think. Too tired, too hungry.

     *Don't cross the bridge. Climb the rutted road instead. Call Denise from the edge of town. Let her come. Let your daughters' songs save you.*

     This voice is soft and sure, not words in Daniel's mind, blood whispering in the vein: *Go home, be warm, be healed.*

     *No!* The dog barks, three hard notes, and the man obeys, crosses the bridge, moves toward him.

     Tejano leaps into Daniel's light, appears and disappears, a dark blur with blond legs—there he is again, rolling in the snow to show his pale belly. He whimpers and whines. *Please come. Please touch me.*

     A whirl of snow,

a dog,

   nothing.

Peter Fleury watches the bouncing beam of light, stays silent and still, safe outside it. Waits to be sure. Yes, the man he knows, the one he wanted.

   *whoo – whoo – whoo*

The frail boy steps into the shivery edge of light. *I think he's here. I think Tejano's found him.*

The dancing dog hears his happy name, pronks three feet off the ground, runs circles around them.

Peter whispers, *Give me the light,*

   leads Daniel to the river's edge,

      flashes the beam down,

         illuminates water.

Yes, here, where the river has carved under the bank, where water runs deep and fast and has not frozen—here, where tangled root grows through dark earth into dark water—they see as owls have seen, hands and feet, eyes not open, a body snagged: a boy taller than Daniel when he walked with Talia. Just today, just this morning. Faster than Peter Fleury when he leaped to save the dog. Amazed when ice cut his face and cold water stunned him.

*Hush now.*

He rocks with the river, raised up by the flow, pulled down by the current, held fast by roots, close to the surface. Snow melts and disappears.

*All one, all nothing. My body knows my blood is water.*

Daniel pulls off coat and gloves, rolls up his sleeves, face flushed hot, poison of adrenaline pumping. He has a knife with six blades, one shaped like a tiny saw, sharp teeth, bright edges. He plunges his hands and arms in cold water, tries to snap a wet root, tugs to pull the boy free, tries to saw with numb fingers.

Tejano yips and prances, delighted by the fierce smell of the man, his strange cries, legs and arms twitching. He steals Daniel's hat, shakes hard and drops it. In love, in frenzy, Tejano nips the man's cold ears, then lies down close to lick him.

Gasping now this pitiful human, crying like the dog, yelps and whimpers rising in his throat, choking him. Peter kneels in the snow. *Please stop.* He touches Daniel's back, presses hard between heaving shoulders. *We can't do this.*

They need an axe, waterproof gloves, ropes to hold—a hook to catch, a sling to lift him.

*How many minutes does the brain live after the heart stops stuttering?*

The man rocks at the edge of the water, knees pulled up to his chest, bare arms clenched around them. The burn of adrenaline leaves its smell but not its fire. Crazy, he knows: cold now, stupid to be this cold for one not living.

*Why are you afraid?*

He remembers lying on Marias Pass, body broken, stars watching.

*When does the last cell flicker and shine, the last nerve spark in utter darkness?*

Peter wraps the coat around him, helps Daniel push numb arms down the sleeves, breathes on the man's curled white hands, pulls padded gloves over bent fingers. *Breath inside of breath, all we are, air swirling.*

Daniel keeps his cell phone zipped tight inside his coat, safe in a secret pocket. His gloved fingers fumble, too thick to work the zipper free. He needs the child to reach inside. *Please.* To call Fire and Rescue. *Yes, here.* To call Tim Dionne, the missing boy's hopeful father.

Peter Fleury—so calm, so patient—lost now three years and finally telling some kind stranger exactly where and how to find him. He keeps his voice low, holds his heart and mind steady. *Do not be distracted.* Describes the narrow bridge, the rutted road. *Unplowed,* he says, but he knows its name, *Tamarack Trail,* and the name of the cleared street, *Swan Loop,* leading to it.

Peter Fleury knows his way down every dirt path and dangerous gully, the whole town mapped in his brain, a maze of bright streets and dark alleys. He knows the dogs who run against their chains, who leap to bite bad boys and fall back choking. He understands the white boxer with one black paw and one black eye who charges his electric fence, jolting through it.

*No fear, no body.* Peter escapes down the steep ravine, crawls on hands and knees through flooded culverts. He sees where the river churns with green silt, cold and tempting. Smells bears deep in caves and reaches one small hand inside to touch them.

One hot day last August, No stole his own bike from his own brother and pedaled fast across the bridge to the end of this road, to a farm where five peacocks strutted in the yard, fanning their miraculous tails. Sapphire blue, turquoise, emerald—every time they turned their colors flickered: copper, gold, green, violet—each feather a huge eye, hundreds of eyes holding him. So small the birds' blue heads, but he knew their luminous minds were in their tails.

Sirens wail at the edge of town.

Peter watches the body of the boy pulled down and caught, rocked by water. *Do not turn away.* He might disappear again, break free somehow and vanish.

Light floods the unplowed road.

These saviors come in trucks with chains, on snowmobiles, in Jeeps and Trackers. *Do not hope. Do not imagine.* Father and uncle appear, Tim Dionne and Roy McKenna. They'll have to walk from the bridge.

*Iris, Neville, Rikki, Trina!* Tejano bounds through snow, throws his body against the children he loves, lost half the day and now recovered.

Headlamps strobe and stun. Snowflakes shatter. The lights of ones walking behind illuminate the ones who lead them. Daniel counts paramedics and firefighters, twelve men who carry hooks and slings, ropes and pulleys—metal jaws with blunt ends—axe, knife, saw, stretcher.

Three men appear dressed in Neoprene—one blazing orange, two brilliant yellow. They wear waterproof gloves, hoods that hide their mouths, boots with crampons. They will not slip, will not give themselves to water. Strapped and harnessed, these three, each one roped and held by two others.

How many children have they found wandering barefoot in the snow or floating down the river? How many bodies have they pried from crushed cars or lifted from soft beds in burning houses? What madness leads a man through smoke and fire?

*Here on earth, their faith is mercy.*

Tomorrow Daniel will learn their names, read their stories in the paper. Reid Kimball and Skeeter Jaynes plunge metal jaws down to hold the body. *My peace is my gift.* Blunted ends close gently. How many times have these two jolted the hearts of the dead and felt the breath return, the pulse flutter? Andre Whitaker chops fast through root. How many times has this man failed? Three firefighters sling the boy as seven men brace to lift him. *And now I rise and now you see me.* Hands bare, clothes dripping. *My body caught in light.* Skin blue and slack, pupils dilated.

*Does God love falling snow less than fireweed or raven?*

No breath, no heartbeat. *Warm air won't open my lungs.* Fifty-one degrees at the core. A probe down the esophagus will tell. *The river is my blood. Nothing you can do will wake me.*

Tonight, tomorrow, forever, Daniel Sidoti will remember two men cutting the boy's clothes to swaddle him in wool and bind him in a silver blanket. *Do you love your own mind? Are your human thoughts so precious?* Until the hour of his own death, Daniel will remember four men carrying the body through the woods, three with light leading the way—thirteen human beings and one silent dog following behind them.

*Here on earth, love is the miracle.*

He'll feel the breath of birds, owls watching.

*Why are you afraid?*

Today a homeless boy spoke to shivering bone. *Hush now.*

In morning light, Peter Fleury heard his real name in his own voice, and then again, in the voice of the river. To the last hour, Peter Fleury believed, *I might be the one to save us.*

Daniel won't remember where or when Peter became No and vanished.

Climbing the hill alone, he imagines a mother touching her drowned son's beautiful feet, amazed to live in a world without him. And a woman who refuses to know where her child is, who never once tried to find him.

Sitting in his truck, fingers too numb to turn the key, Daniel Sidoti remembers lying on Marias Pass, wondering if he would know when he died, if he might be dead already. Remembers the car passing very slowly, pulling to the side of the road. That unbelievable burst of light. Doors on both sides opening. *Human voices.* Two women kneeling in the snow, mother and daughter holding him now, warm breath hovering above his body. They spoke in whisper and sigh, soft sweet murmur and moan. *Love, only love.* Their breath became his breath. The heat of their blood pulsed through him.

He's afraid to go home, to be loved by ones he loves, to feel small hands on cold skin, to see Clare and Nora as he did last night, gold light of the hall glowing behind them, light touching them so tenderly, *not yours to keep,* gold light illuminating pale nightgowns, bodies becoming air, *each one, once only—Kai, Peter, Clare, Nora,* these children in their rags of light, fragile bones almost visible.

## 20

## THE MIRACLE

*Lullaby for Lost Children*

In wildering, wet spring, the black bear leads her cubs from the dark den into the miraculous light of a new world.

Pink pyrola, trailing daisy—bees, frogs, flying squirrels— white bark of weeping birch, yellow limbs of weeping willow. Buds of the cherry glow; hawthorn breaks to bright blossom. Porcupine, lynx, skunk, weasel—magenta flames of shooting stars, brilliant gold of glacier lilies.

*Hush now, belovéd.*

The low limbs of fir have taken root beneath snow, and now new shoots rise: thin stalks delicate as grass, silky needles soft as feathers. Pine, spruce, tamarack, cedar: everything alive, new and green, a blaze of green, morning light through fine new needles. The aspen survives fire and drought, saw and poison. Its leaves quiver with light. Its body feeds deer, elk, moose, beaver—goat, grouse, rabbit, quail. A grove of five hundred trees is one being, one root beneath this earth tangled. This root holds back soil and stone. This grove saves the river. The oxygen these trees breathe out to air restores the world.

*Why are you afraid?*

The hummingbird comes to sip from foxglove and Sweet William, drinks from the hollyhock, opens the snapdragon. The smallest poppies bloom rose and scarlet, opening themselves to light, waving illuminated hearts in a bed of violet iris.

*All life is love.*

> Bluebirds sing before dawn
> as if light
> shimmers in their throats
> and day rises from them.

One brilliant tanager swoops tree to tree, gold and orange, black-winged, silent. Hundreds of snow geese pass, a thousand feet above the world.

*What more evidence do you need?*

Snow melts into dark earth and here in damp woods white trillium blossoms. Seven years since these seeds sprouted, and now for the first time they flower. Beautiful as the face of God: three white petals open. Slanted rays of sun glint through high branches, but rarely touch them. Here they thrive. Close to earth, close to darkness. Seen but not trampled by the elk whose body feeds wolf and bear, fox and raven.

*River, cloud, birch, aspen—do you love only what returns love, or have you learned to love stone and silence?*

The tiny hermit thrush hiding deep in these woods holds one radiant note so sweet and clear it seems the bird will shatter—and then it does shatter: into a heart-sparking ripple of song that echoes tree to tree and leaves the earth trembling.

## ACKNOWLEDGMENTS

I am grateful to the Lannan Foundation for providing sanctuary and support in Marfa, Texas. I am also grateful to the National Endowment for the Arts; Corby Skinner and the Writer's Voice Project in Billings, Montana; the Utah Arts Council; Bob Goldberg and the Tanner Humanities Center; and the University of Utah, especially Dean Robert Newman and the College of Humanities. The faith of these individuals and the support of these institutions have made my work possible. Thank you.

I thank my family for their unwavering belief, their extraordinary contributions to research, their joyful reading and patient listening. Dear Gary, Glenna, Laurie, Wendy, Tom, Melinda, Kelsey, Chris, Mike, Sam, Brad, Hayley—Dear Mom, dear Father even now—Dear Cleora, Randy, Alicia, Valerie, Kimmer, Kristi—Dear Jan and John: without your love, there are no stories. Thank you.

To my students who shatter all opinions and challenge all assumptions, thank you.

The blessing of my agent Irene Skolnick's friendship and dedication has upheld me for twenty-five years. I am also indebted to Erin Harris for her generosity and commitment. Thank you.

To the editors of the journals where stories and poems from this novel first appeared—*Five Points, Agni, Indiana Review,*

*Conjunctions, Virginia Quarterly Review, Glimmer Train, Short Fiction, Southern Review, Iron Horse Literary Review, On Earth As It Is, Crazyhorse, Image: A Journal of the Arts and Religion, StoryQuarterly, Antioch Review, and Idaho Review*—thank you.

I am grateful to Carmen Edington, Lou Robinson, the board members and staff of FC2, Carole Maso, Daniel Waterman, and to the entire staff at University of Alabama Press. Thank you.

Many friends have sustained me on the journey of this novel. Kate Coles, Christine Flanagan, Caz Phillips, Mary Pinard, Miles Coiner, Matthew Archibald, Eric Shapiro, Don Engelman, Janet Kaufman, Diedre Kindsfather, Leigh Gilmore, Lauren Abramson, Alice Lichtenstein, Michael Martone, Vonnie Mahugh Day, Glenn and Ginnie Walters, John Vaillant, Erin McGraw, Margot Rogers Calabrese, Bruce Hilliard, Ruth Anderson, Annea Lockwood, Sheila Moss, Diana Joseph, Beth Domholdt, Margaret Himley, Jane Marie Law, David Gewanter, Reesie Johnson, Barbara Painter, Mark Robbins, Mary Tabor, Betsy Burton, Matthew and Jenae Batt, Bruce Machart, Randy Schwickert, Larry Cooper, Halina Duraj, Katy Ryan, David McGlynn, Stephanie Matlak, Matthew Pelikan, Jill Patterson, Megan Sexton, Joel Long, Pam Balluck, Lance and Andi Olsen: dear friends, for your love and companionship, inspiration and insight, for reading with joy and contributing to research, I thank you.